"The only way this green-card marriage will work is if we pretend that we are in love."

Molly let go of a long, shaky breath. "Can you pretend to be wildly in love with me?

Alejandro inclined his head, and she felt his gaze slide over her hair, touch her breasts, her hands. Mockingly, he pursed his lips, as if considering. Sighing heavily, he said, "Well, I will try."

She gave him a faint smile. "You're teasing me."

He laughed, and it occurred to her that she had not heard that sound before. It rolled from his chest, as welcome as desert rain. He moved close and held out a hand to her. "Should we…try to see if we can do it?"

"What do you mean?"

He stepped close, lifting his hands to her face. "Practice?"

Before she could protest, Alejandro pressed that beautiful mouth to hers.

Dear Reader,

What is there to say about a month with a new Nora Roberts title except "Hurry up and get to the store!" *Enchanted* is a mysterious, romantic and utterly irresistible follow-up to THE DONOVAN LEGACY trilogy, which appeared several years ago and is currently being reissued. It's the kind of story only Nora can tell—and boy, will you be glad she did!

The rest of our month is pretty special, too, so pick up a few more books to keep you warm. Try *The Admiral's Bride,* by Suzanne Brockmann, the latest TALL, DARK & DANGEROUS title. These navy SEAL heroes are fast staking claim to readers' hearts all over the world. Read about the last of THE SISTERS WASKOWITZ in Kathleen Creighton's *Eve's Wedding Knight.* You'll love it—and you'll join me in hoping we revisit these fascinating women—and their irresistible heroes—someday. *Rio Grande Wedding* is the latest from multiaward-winning Ruth Wind, a part of her MEN OF THE LAND miniseries, featuring the kind of Southwestern men no self-respecting heroine can resist. Take a look at Vickie Taylor's *Virgin Without a Memory,* a book *you'll* remember for a long time. And finally, welcome Harlequin Historical author Mary McBride to the contemporary romance lineup. *Just One Look* will demand more than just one look from you, and it will have you counting the days until she sets another story in the present day.

And, of course, mark your calendar and come back next month, when Silhouette Intimate Moments will once again bring you six of the most excitingly romantic novels you'll ever find.

Enjoy!

Leslie J. Wainger

Leslie J. Wainger
Executive Senior Editor

Please address questions and book requests to:
Silhouette Reader Service
U.S.: 3010 Walden Ave., P.O. Box 1325, Buffalo, NY 14269
Canadian: P.O. Box 609, Fort Erie, Ont. L2A 5X3

RIO GRANDE WEDDING

RUTH WIND

Silhouette

INTIMATE™MOMENTS®

Published by Silhouette Books

America's Publisher of Contemporary Romance

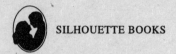

SILHOUETTE BOOKS

ISBN 0-373-07964-8

RIO GRANDE WEDDING

Copyright © 1999 by Barbara Samuel

Visit us at www.romance.net

Printed in U.S.A.

Books by Ruth Wind

Silhouette Intimate Moments

Silhouette Special Edition

*The Last Roundup
†Men of the Land

RUTH WIND

is the award-winning author of both contemporary and historical romance novels. She lives in the mountains of the Southwest with her husband, two growing sons and many animals in a hundred-year-old house the town blacksmith built. The only hobby she has since she started writing is tending the ancient garden of irises, lilies and lavender beyond her office window, and she says she can think of no more satisfying way to spend a life than growing children, books and flowers.

This one is for the community of Genie RomEx,
which has given me thousands of hours of thoughtful
discussion, probing insights and great laughs.
Thanks, guys.

Prologue

The old women always said there was a face carved upon the heart of every woman. A face half remembered on a hundred sun-glazed afternoons spent daydreaming in classrooms that smelled of chalk, a face that haunted her on nights when the full moon shone into her sweet-smelling virgin bedroom. A face mostly forgotten as husband, children, work came to take her time.

Mostly forgotten.

But the old women told each other stories of those times when a woman glimpsed that face in a crowd of strangers, crowds like those at the chile festival, or the rodeo held in the dog days of August, crowds so large that face quickly became lost. Such women sometimes sickened, for once glimpsed, the face of her destino came clear and haunted her forever.

Worse were the times when the face suddenly appeared next door or on the arm of a cousin, and it was worn by a man married to another or chained by duty to the Church. Of such tragedies were crimes of passion made. That face, the old women said, was the reason women left husbands who had been good to them for fifteen, twenty, fifty years, because when that face appeared, she was helpless to halt the lure of it. It was the reason women sometimes did crazy things— loco!—that everyone clucked about over pots of steaming tamales.

Clucked, yes, but sighed, too, their eyes raised to the misty distance, for who among them did not hope, secretly, to find that face, no matter where it lived on the earth, what upheaval it caused? It was better, they all thought privately, if one never knew she was waiting. If she was never tempted.

But it did not stop her from looking.

Chapter 1

Molly Sheffield stepped out onto her back steps, a mug of steaming coffee clutched in her hands. It was half past six in the morning, the freshest part of the day, and Molly wouldn't think of drinking her first cup of coffee anywhere else when the weather was fine.

Above, the sky brightened with sunrise. Pure gold light, gentle and clear, seeped into the bowl of endless sky, tipping the wings of a pair of magpies swooping over the silhouette of cottonwoods that marked the eastern edge of her nearly one hundred acres.

When her husband, Tim, died four years ago, this view, morning and evening, had often saved her sanity. There was, in the vast stillness, a sense of eternity that comforted her.

Everyone had said she would recover, and to her surprise, Molly had—more or less. It had happened gradually, but now she could stand on this square of porch her husband had built with his own hands, and

face the austere bluffs to the north and watch the sun
rise with a genuine sense of deep pleasure, unblunted
by sorrow. She missed him still, of course, the way one
would miss an amputated arm, but the phantom pains
grew less frequent with every passing month. She knew
he'd be glad.

As the fingers of buttery light crept into her garden,
Molly ambled down the rock path she'd laid by herself
last summer. A pink and yellow rose, sturdily blooming
in the unseasonably warm October, opened dewy petals
to the day. Molly took a moment to bend close and
smell the faintly citrusy scent, then headed up the narrow path that wound beneath piñon, juniper and cedar
trees to the top of the bluff that was the northern
boundary of her land.

From some hidden spot came the sound of a family
of wrens, singing over breakfast, and one of the magpies from the cottonwoods dived toward his favorite
perch, scolding noisily. Molly smiled and saw her cat,
Leonardo, flatten himself apprehensively beneath a
lavender plant.

''Scaredy-cat,'' she said. He made a soft trill in answer. He didn't spend much time outside because of
the threat of coyotes, and as a result, he was jumpy
when he did.

A flash of something bright caught her eye as she
turned toward the bluff in the distance, and Molly
paused, blinded for a second. She squinted and held up
her hand to block the light. Probably a piece of glass.
She moved toward it, worried that one of the animals
that foraged around here might cut a paw on it.

Five feet away, she stopped dead.

The light was not catching on a piece of glass. It
was an oblong silver medal, attached to a chain that

hung around the neck of a man. A man who was either dead or unconscious at the bottom of the steep bluff.

Her land bordered an enormous farm that depended on an army of migrant workers to bring in the harvest of chiles, peaches and cantaloupe that grew in such abundance in the mild northern New Mexico highlands. As Molly edged closer to the man, she decided he must be a member of that army, mostly Mexican nationals. He wore their uniform—a simple white tank top and jeans, and his skin showed the deep tan of a man who worked outside every day.

He was sprawled on his back. Red dust clouded one arm, part of his side and his legs, as if he'd slipped and skidded all the way down the bluff. A large red stain of blood soaked the denim of his left leg.

But it was his face that drew her closer, and between one step and another, she felt an odd, piercing stab of apprehension, as if she should stay where she was, run away, turn back while she had a chance.

For it was the most singularly perfect face she had ever seen. Not perfect in terms of photographs or movie stars. The angles were too sharp, his nose too aggressive, his mouth too wide for those things.

But as she knelt, the trained nurse cataloguing his obvious wounds, she found herself thinking that if she'd drawn the face of a man, if she'd had the talent to paint someone into existence, her man would have worn this dark and sensual face. She would have used these strong colors, his flesh the reddish copper of the earth itself, his hair and eyebrows like the tail feathers of the magpies sweeping overhead. She would have painted his lashes just so, luxuriant against the arch of bone in his cheek, and used a generous hand with the mouth because the softness in such a hard face pleased her.

Yes, if her skill equaled her heart's eye, which it did not, she would have painted this man for herself.

Her cat crept up to the downed man, sniffing with worry and curiosity, his extraordinarily long whiskers wiggling, his yellow eyes wide and bright. When the man shifted slightly and let out a low noise, Leonardo jumped a foot in the air and bolted for the house.

It shook Molly from her daze, and with a frown, she ticked off his wounds—the face was bruised and very dirty, and one cheekbone showed a long scrape, giving credence to her theory of a fall down the bluff.

She glanced upward. Maybe thirty feet. It wouldn't be hard to fall if he'd been up there at night—he might not even have seen the drop in time to do anything to stop himself. The desert on a moonless night was a very dark place indeed.

There must have been a raid at the farms last night. Not an unusual occurrence. In his flight, this man must have missed seeing the abrupt end of land, and tumbled down the bluff.

She looked back at him, assessing. No limbs at odd angles. No visible head injury—he'd probably taken a bullet to that leg, and passed out from loss of blood. He—or someone—had packed grass and mud into the wound. Molly half shuddered at the likelihood of infection, but the move had probably saved his life.

For the moment, anyway.

Her training did not allow the option of simply leaving him there while she called for an ambulance. She rose from her crouch a few feet away and stepped forward; the sound of her feet or maybe the shadow of her body falling on him made the man stir.

Barely. He made a low noise of pain, and his head moved as Molly knelt next to him. "Can you hear me?" she said, and touched his forehead. Definitely feverish.

His eyes opened as she reached for his wrist to take his pulse, and he started, protesting in mumbled Spanish so jumbled Molly couldn't make out the words.

"Shh," she murmured, and put her finger on his wrist, automatically looking at her watch to count the beats. Not bad. "You're hurt. I need to get you an ambulance."

"No!" His hand gripped hers with surprising fierceness. "No, *señora. Por favor.* No hospital." He licked his lips. "I have to find Josefina." His eyes were as dark as coffee. "She is alone," he said. "Please—no hospital." He gripped her hand urgently. "Please."

If she needed additional proof that he'd been running from a raid last night, that cinched it. If she called an ambulance, the authorities would be alerted and he'd be deported.

"Can you walk?" she asked, choosing to sidestep the request. "With my help? I'm a nurse. Maybe I can look at the wound myself."

He swallowed. *"Sí."*

He struggled to sit up, but the strong ropes of muscle across his arms and chest were little help to him now. A ghastly grayness bled the color from his face, and Molly bent down, looped his arm around her neck and anchored it with one hand. Bracing herself on her thighs, she locked the other arm around his waist. She was accustomed to assisting barely mobile patients, but this was not a small man—he was a solid six-two and even though he was a little thin, she'd guess a hundred and eighty pounds of the kind of wiry muscle farmwork gave a man.

They staggered a little together before he found some steadiness. A choked noise of pain came from his throat before he could swallow it, and the effort of standing made him tremble from shoulder to hip.

Molly braced her body against the ground and held on. She waited for him to catch his breath, thinking of the Josefina he couldn't leave behind. A wife? A child?

"Ready?" she asked quietly when the trembling had eased a little.

He gave her a grim nod. Inch by inch, they made it down the last yard of slope, into the level garden. She watched his face for signs of impending disaster, but though his color remained gray, and sweat beaded his lip and forehead, he managed to stay upright and struggle toward the house. By the time she got him inside to the living-room couch, he was trembling visibly, and she didn't think she had long before he passed out entirely.

"*Señor,*" she said urgently, breathing hard with effort. "Who are you looking for?"

His breath was ragged and he clutched his leg. "She ran...when the..." He blinked, and swayed dangerously, but she saw the finely cut jaw tense, and after a moment, he said, "When the *migra* came." He closed his eyes, and the cords on his neck showed the struggle he mounted to speak at all. "*Dios!*" he whispered, a voice broken with worry and love, and he squeezed his eyes shut. "Josefina."

It pierced her. "Shh," she said instinctively. "Lie down. Let me help you."

She pushed him sideways, and he went down, half whispering in Spanish she suspected would be incoherent even if she were fluent, which she was not. She knew enough to get answers for medical charts, to soothe a frantic patient or mother or brother, enough to get a woman through childbirth. In a county where most of the farm labor was supplied by migrant workers, and where at least half of the local population had been speaking Spanish among themselves for more than four hundred years, she'd had to learn at least that much.

Efficiently, she began to assess his wounds as he lost consciousness. She knew what she ought to be doing—calling an ambulance, pronto. But his repeated pleas had moved her. If she could take care of him without putting him in physical danger, she felt obliged to give him that chance. What if this had been her late husband, Tim, in a foreign place, and he'd been looking for Molly?

She'd been a nurse for more than ten years, and had treated more than her share of traumas. Deftly, she cut his jeans with a pair of heavy scissors, straight up the leg, and exposed the wound with its primitive but effective packing of mud and grass. Carefully, she removed it, surprised when it held together, like a flat adobe pancake.

Beneath the packing was the bullet wound she'd expected. Molly swore mildly. Using a fresh dish towel, she blotted it clean and spied what she was looking for—the round end of a bullet, lodged—thank God—not far from the surface. He'd been lucky—not only had the bullet missed the bone, but it was something Molly could handle.

Thankful for her patient's unconsciousness, she gathered a pile of clean cloths, water and alcohol for sterilization, then quickly removed the bullet and disin-

fected the injury. Not unexpectedly, there was heat and
redness around the wound, signs of infection.
"Damn," she muttered. Wincing in sympathy, she
cleaned the area with alcohol and covered it with a
thick, sterile gauze.

"Gracias," he said gruffly, startling her.

Molly looked up in surprise. That had not been a
painless procedure, and she wondered how he'd managed to remain still and silent. "Do you hurt anywhere
else?" she asked in Spanish, and touched his ribs.
"Here?"

A reflexive grunt of pain and a nod. The grayness
had come back around his lips.

"I'm sorry," she said. "Did you hit your head when
you fell?"

"No."

"Good." No concussion, then. He'd probably
passed out from exhaustion and loss of blood. Likely
he'd lost quite a bit before he'd fallen. Briskly, she
stood and changed the water in the basin, and returned
with a fresh cloth. When she knelt beside him, he
opened his eyes once more. "I'm only going to wash
your face," she said, this time in English.

He nodded slightly and closed his eyes.

Molly lifted the cloth to wipe dust from his forehead,
and again she felt that sense of warning and fierce attraction, so sharp it made her hesitate. She almost felt
she remembered this face, that it had lurked somewhere
in the back of her mind, glimpsed only in dreams.

Give me a break, said a scoffing voice in her mind.
Molly half smiled and gently swabbed the long scrape
on his cheekbone. Raw but not deep. She wondered
vaguely if it would scar.

"Done," she said, dropping the rag. "Rest here for

a little—I don't think you're going anywhere for at
least a few hours.''

But she said it for her own benefit. Her patient was
out cold. For a moment, she hesitated, thinking she
probably should call the hospital. Or even the sheriff—
if her brother, Josh, discovered that she'd hidden an
alien in her house, he'd be fit to be tied.

At the thought of her brother, tension drew up her
shoulders. It served the purpose of grounding her again
in reality—what in the world did she think she was
doing? His fear of going to the hospital proved the
wounded man was either a criminal or a migrant
worker in fear of deportation, and though she was
pretty sure it was the latter, what if it was the former?
Either way, her brother would see it as aiding and abetting a fugitive.

And yet, even as she moved toward the phone, she
was oddly hesitant.

Josh was the biggest worry. A deputy sheriff who
took his job seriously—too seriously for Molly's tastes
at times—he would be very upset with her if he discovered she'd done something like this. It wouldn't
even be a matter of the legalities involved—he simply
saw the world in black-and-white terms, and couldn't
understand the gray areas that existed for most people.

The other worry—that the man might be badly injured—she'd just alleviated. She could call an ambulance and they'd come and get him, take him to the
hospital for a day or two, then ship him home. But they
wouldn't be doing anything more for him physically
than giving him a clean bed to rest in and some antibiotics to clear the infection.

That left the danger factor. Although he was in no
shape to be a threat at the moment, Molly didn't know

anything about his character, after all. He could be a murderer or a drug runner or any number of unsavory other things.

Still undecided, she picked up the handset.

As if sensitive to her thoughts, the man stirred and whispered, in a broken, anguished fashion, a single name. "Josefina!"

Molly put the phone down. He was exactly what he appeared to be, a Mexican national migrant worker who'd run from a raid. A man who was anguished over being separated from a beloved other. A man injured enough that he was no threat to her—at least at the moment.

"Oh, really, Molly," she said aloud. "Be honest."

It was that face, manifesting right out of her most private imaginings, that halted her. He moved her. Physically, as in hormonal, as in she had forgotten what that sudden, pleasurable swoop of sexual attraction could feel like. He had the long-limbed body she most liked on a man, and the healthy, lean strength that came from working the land. His hair, black as licorice and slightly curly, was a bit too long and a little untamed. Sexy. Such great eyes, too, so dark and deep, full of depths Molly had been amazed to find herself wanting to explore. Even glazed as they'd been with pain and confusion, she had seen the intensity lurking there, a fire and intelligence that was very compelling.

She smiled to herself. Okay, so maybe she wouldn't be so quick to be on his side if he was short and stout. So what?

But even beyond that, she hesitated because of the worry and love she heard in his voice when he called out Josefina's name. In her view, devotion should be rewarded, not punished.

It couldn't hurt to shelter him until he had healed enough to find his lost Josefina. Molly couldn't turn him away or turn him in until then. If things went well enough, her brother would never even have to know what she'd done.

The tension of indecision melted away, and she went to the kitchen to slice tomatoes, forming a plan to resolve the situation before it became troublesome. Later, maybe she'd go to town and have lunch at the Navajo Café. Listen to the gossip—maybe she'd hear a clue. After that, she could swing by the hospital and check on new arrivals.

Later, though. She was a little worried about her patient, and didn't want to leave him alone until he seemed stable.

In the meantime, she called her best friend and Josh's wife, Lynette. To stay abreast of his activities, Lynette kept a scanner on twenty-four hours a day. Molly found it a little gruesome to listen to the conversation of ambulance attendants or the shouts echoing in the background at a domestic-violence call, but she could understand Lynette's need to be sure her husband was safe. She would also know exactly what had happened last night at Wiley Farms.

When Lynette answered, she sounded breathless and annoyed. "Hello?"

"Hey, sis," Molly said, smiling. In the background, she heard the sound of her eight-year-old niece howling mournfully. "Rough day?"

A heartfelt sigh. "Two cases of the flu. Are we on for lunch today?"

"Did we have plans? I was going to dry tomatoes."

"I know. You can't blame a girl for trying. I've had about as much as I can stand of kids throwing up. I finally got them both in school full-time, and now this.''

Molly chuckled. "Won't be long. Let's make a date for next week, huh?"

"You got it." She spoke in a murmuring aside to one of the children, then asked, "What's up?"

"I thought I heard something last night." A lie, but it might have been true. "Was there trouble at the orchards?"

"A raid," Lynette said. "Josh was there. Said they rounded up about thirty illegals, I guess. Wiley is fit to be tied—says he can't get his crop in without that help."

"Mmm." Molly looked at the man on the couch. His black hair fell over his face and neck like a spill of cloth. "Did they get all of them?"

"Pretty much. Jake Arnott chased one into an arroyo, but he got away, and there were probably a couple of others. You know they never get everybody." A pause. "Why?"

"I was just curious. I thought I heard gunfire."

"They don't shoot them, Moll. Must have been your imagination. I keep telling you to get a dog. Then you wouldn't be so jumpy."

"You're right. Thanks. I just wondered what was going on out there."

A sudden burst of tears sounded on the other end of the line. With another harried sigh, Lynette said, "I gotta go."

"Okay. Don't forget, next week, you'll be free again."

"If I live that long."

Molly chuckled. "You will."

* * *

Alejandro Sosa awakened slowly, an inch of his body at a time. Unfortunately, the painful parts awakened first—the pulled muscles across his chest, the scrape on his face and the roaring in his leg. He struggled to the surface, and found himself making an unmanly noise of pain.

"Easy," said a woman's voice. A hand fell on his shoulder.

He opened his eyes. The woman was the same one who had appeared in the garden. A gentle face with a firm mouth and high cheekbones that gave her an exotic look. Gray eyes. An impression of long hair with brown and yellow stripes weaving through the braid.

She knelt beside him, eyes concerned but not suspicious. *"¿Cómo está usted?"* she asked.

Abruptly he remembered where he was—and why. He bolted upright, sending waves of agony from his thigh to his gut, and he put a hand to the bolt of pain in his head.

Cursing softly, he willed himself to sit there without showing his pain or the waves of nausea washing over him. To his disgust, his hand trembled. He lowered it and forced himself to speak evenly. "I have to find Josefina," he said in English, so there would be no question of her understanding. "Please. I have to go."

Her hand pushed him—all too easily—back against the soft couch. "You can't even sit up yet." She rocked back on her heels and Alejandro liked the strength in her features, the no-nonsense way she met his eyes. "I might be able to help if you tell me who she is, how I might recognize her."

Could he trust her? He looked at the room behind her, darkened by twilight. It was clean and simply furnished, with plants in groups around the windows and a painting of the mountains over the fireplace. Even that small survey, moving only his eyes, brought fresh waves of dizziness, and he let his head fall into his waiting hands, breathing slow and deep to stall the nausea. *"Madre,"* he whispered.

Her cool hand lit on his forehead, and she swore softly. "Look, I want to move you to a more comfortable bed. Do you think you can walk a little way?"

"No, no." It was dark. He could not bear to think of Josefina out there, alone and afraid, hiding until he could find her. "I must go."

A tightness marked her mouth, and she stepped back. "Go ahead. Give it your best."

Alejandro worked his way to a full sitting position and halted, waiting for the dizziness to subside. He was a strong man. Healthy. He did not drink spirits or weaken himself with tobacco. In all his life, he had never been ill, not even with a cold. In a moment, his head would clear and he would stand up, and though it would hurt, he would leave here and find Josefina.

But he waited, and the dizziness did not abate. He felt his head drifting above his body somewhere, above the dull, steady throb of his leg. Suddenly, nausea flared in his belly and he swayed, feeling cold sweat break on his forehead and down his back. He closed his eyes, fighting it, but found himself resting his face in his hands.

"Señor," she said quietly. "Have a little water."

She pressed a glass into his hand, and to his shame, had to help him lift it to his lips. The taste was cool and sweet against his parched lips, however, and he drank greedily. His stomach settled and he nodded.

The woman put the glass aside and put a strong hand

on his elbow. "You have been shot. Was it in the raid last night at Wiley Farms?"

He met her gaze. If she knew that, and still listened to his plea to keep the officials out of it, she was not likely to care if he told the truth now. *"Sí."*

"There's infection in the wound, which is what is making you so ill. I can get some antibiotics and you'll be better in a couple of days, but in the meantime, you aren't going to be able to walk more than a few feet without falling on your face. Not on an infected, gunshot leg." She paused. "Let me help you."

Even in his present state, he was bewildered by her kindness. "Why?"

Her eyebrows lifted. "I don't really know." Gripping his elbow, she said, "Let's get you settled. Then you can tell me what I need to know to help locate Josefina."

He had no choice. He nodded.

"Can you stand up? There is a more comfortable bed in the back room."

He hoped so. Bracing himself, Alejandro gritted his teeth as he leaned on her. Even with her help, it took every shred of his will to move the short distance to a bedroom off the kitchen. He noted windows all around, and a swept wooden floor and a lamp burning warmly in one corner before he eased into the comfort of the clean, fresh-smelling linens. Blackness edged his vision, and he took her hand urgently, to speak before unconsciousness claimed him again.

"Señora," he said urgently, and paused to gather the English words.

"I'm here." Her hand was strong. Reliable, somehow.

She bent over him in that way of caretakers, moving

into his view so he did not have to even turn his head.
As he gathered his words, he saw that she had a face
like a saint, that smooth white skin, and heaven-soft
eyes, and a long rope of brown and yellow hair that
shone in the light.

"Tell me about Josefina," she said in Spanish, as if
realizing what effort it took for him to concentrate.

"I lost her in the raid, and she is ill." He tried to
remember what else. "She's...little. *Ocho años.*"

"*Su hija?*"

"No, no." Blackness crept over him. "My niece....
por favor."

"I'll find her," she promised, and squeezed his
hand.

Believing her, he let go and blackness swarmed over
him, velvety and deep and free of pain.

Molly felt his grip loosen as he slipped into the fever. She settled his lean dark hand on his belly, then
efficiently removed his boots—an act that would have
been agonizing for him while he was conscious—then
found her scissors and cut away his jeans completely
so that he could rest more comfortably. She'd made the
bed before she moved him, and now braced the
wounded leg between two pillows to help keep it im-
mobile. Though the evening was not cold, she covered
him with a light quilt, anticipating the chill a fever
sometimes brought with it.

Fever. She needed antibiotics. There were some
painkillers in a bottle in the medicine cabinet, left over
from dental surgery a few months ago, and when he
could eat a little, she'd give him those. But the need
for antibiotics was urgent. His temperature was up, and

the leg was burning. The last thing in the world she wanted was to end up with a dead man in her house.

She pulled another light blanket over him, tucking it around him loosely so he'd stay warm but would not feel constrained. Again, the impossible beauty of his face struck her. Wounded and ill as he was, his face was still so astonishing Molly couldn't help staring. Such artful lines.

And not only his face. The body was lean, hard-muscled, tan. She had a weakness for men who worked the land, who spent their days in the sun, touching what grew or roamed on the earth. In her experience, it didn't matter whether it was a lowly field hand or a rancher with hundreds of acres, men of the land were a breed apart. They looked to the sky and tasted the wind and knew they were at the mercy of nature. It lent them humility and dignity.

Her husband had been such a man. For a moment, she thought of the fan of sun lines that had marked Tim's face by the time he was thirty, and waited for a hollow ache such memories usually brought. This time, it did not come. She felt only fondness.

Although her patient would not likely stir for many hours, she left a small pitcher of water on the nightstand, along with a cup. There was a small bathroom across the hall, probably reachable if he held on to walls, and she left the light on to lead the way if he awakened.

Then she set out to see if she could make good on her promise to find Josefina, trying in vain to ignore the pleasure she felt over discovering it was not his wife, but a child, that her patient called for with such devotion.

Chapter 2

Josefina knew two things about the world—that people usually liked little girls as long as they were polite, and that she got better results from grandmothers. She had been hiding all day, waiting for her uncle to come find her, but as the sun set, she got hungrier and hungrier, and finally decided to take a chance.

It was good for her that she did not look so different from many of the girls in this town. They were dark, like her, and skinny, and some of them even spoke their English in the same way she did. The teachers liked it crisper—a teacher in camp last summer had said that, *crisper,* and Josefina had loved the sound of it. Like lettuce, she had said with a laugh, and the teacher had laughed with her. So now she tried to remember to break the words like lettuce, but sometimes she forgot.

Tonight, she had on her good blue sweater, because it had been chilly last night, and a pair of jeans with the shirt that had a big sunflower on it that Tío had bought her for her birthday.

There weren't so many people out, but Josefina halted outside the pool of light near the dairy bar, looking for more bad men. She didn't see any. Mostly there were teenagers, who scared her a little with their loud laughing and flat eyes. Sometimes they were nice, but mostly they looked through her.

In her pocket, she had ten dollars. She always had it, just in case, Tío said, and he'd made her think about how to buy things and get the right change so many times she felt confident walking up to the window now to get herself some supper. Soberly, she thought of her choices. They had hot dogs and ice-cream cones on special for $1.75, and she ordered that, then carefully counted the change and tucked it back in her pocket, coughing a little.

Then a lot. The cough doubled her over for a minute, and she felt tiny stabbing pains in her chest. It wouldn't go away. It was always worse in the nighttime. The people at the clinic said it was asthma, and had given her a little thing to breathe with. She took it out of her pocket and used it, and it helped a little. The lady behind the counter frowned a little and asked her if she was sick.

"I'm okay," Josefina assured her. "Just asthma."

She couldn't carry the food all the way back to the orchard, so she took a chance and found a dark corner behind the dairy bar to sit and eat. Nobody bothered her. Nobody probably even saw her, except a little dog with raggedy fur who was so polite about begging that she saved the last bit of hot dog, then the last bite of ice cream, and gave them both to him. She was happy when he followed her.

He was warm next to her when she went back to the deserted part of the orchard where she'd slept the night before. And she didn't feel so scared with him sleeping along her stomach. Once he growled softly, and that made her happiest of all. He'd wake her up barking if the bad men came back.

In the morning, surely Tío would find her.

Molly knew she wasn't a good liar. There had never been much need for subterfuge in her life, after all, and it took practice to be good at something. Still, she thought as she approached the café, she needed a good excuse to ask the questions she had to ask, so she made up a story.

The Navajo Café had started as a dark little hole in the wall catering to bus passengers who had a meal stop in Vallejos. Over the years, the restaurant had doubled, then tripled its original size. A cowbell over the door rang as Molly went in, and she waved to several friendly faces as she made her way to the counter. "Hi, Maureen," she said to the waitress as she sat down. "Coffee, please."

"Special today is black-bean burritos," Maureen said, turning over a heavy ceramic cup. "Soup is corn chowder."

"Soup, please." She glanced around casually. "Not too busy tonight, is it?" Across the room, she saw a familiar face, bent over a stack of papers, his blond hair tousled, as if he'd had his hands in it again. His regulation tie was loose. "Take it to my brother's table," she said, swinging off the stool.

"Will do, hon."

Josh, absorbed in whatever paperwork he had stacked up, didn't notice her, and for a minute, Molly was torn over the reality of what she was about to do. He looked exhausted, and that made her feel guilty. Unfortunately, she also knew he brought a lot of exhaustion on himself. Three years younger than she, twenty-seven to her thirty, he was honorable and loving, but also dogmatic and hard to live with sometimes. She kept hoping he'd grow into a little compassion, but it hadn't happened yet. He followed the straight and narrow, and expected the rest of the world to follow suit.

"Hi, stranger," she said, sliding into the booth.

He looked up, taking a minute to focus on her face. "Molly!" He scrambled to move some of the forms to give her room. "What's going on? Everything okay?"

"Fine." She helped him stack some of the papers into a pile. "Why are you still working so late?"

He put his hand in his hair, leaving it sticking up on top. "Can't seem to catch up."

Molly reached over the table and smoothed the pointy lock back down. "You should be home with Lynette by now."

"I can't get anything done there. I called her." His blue eyes lowered. "I feel bad, but the kids are just wired at night."

Molly almost offered to baby-sit so they could go out alone together this weekend, then remembered the secret asleep in her back room. "Hang in there, kiddo," she said. "They'll be asking for the keys to the car any minute."

He tossed the pencil down. "Don't remind me."

"Have you eaten?"

"Nah. Just wanted to spend an hour away from all the distractions to see if I could make some progress here." He gestured toward the pile in front of him.

"This is paperwork from that raid last night. I don't know why the hell we had to process every—" He gave her a rueful smile. "Never mind."

"I'll buy you some supper," she said, carefully not looking at the papers. Whatever she discovered had to be pure gossip between siblings. "A steak?"

"I can't let you do that, Molly."

"Don't be silly." He was supporting a family of four on the mediocre salary of a deputy sheriff. Molly not only had her job at the hospital as a floor nurse, but a sizable insurance settlement from Tim's death. He'd left her, if not rich, at least moderately well-to-do.

But she still had to bully her brother into taking so much as a quarter from her. When Maureen brought her coffee, Molly said, "Bring Josh the New York steak, please, and put it on my check."

"Got it." She took out her green ticket book and scribbled the order.

When the waitress left, Molly decided to get business out of the way first. "I'm glad to see you here, actually. I was going to call you later. Maybe you'll know about a little girl."

He frowned. "What?"

Molly took a deep breath, wondering what people did with their eyes when they weren't lying. The edges of her mouth felt stiff, but she said, "There was a little girl who used to come see me every morning, from the orchards."

He still looked puzzled. "What about her?"

"Did you guys pick her up last night? She didn't come to see me this morning." The lie was feeling a little less troublesome now. In her imagination, Molly could see a skinny eight-year-old with long black hair sitting in her garden. "I'm worried about her."

"You should know better than to get attached to those kids."

She nodded, smiling apologetically. "I know, but she's pretty cute. About eight. Her name is Josefina." She stirred her coffee. "Ring any bells?"

And just before he answered, Molly panicked. What if he asked what she looked like? She had no idea. Her heart actually pinched, and a ripple of radiating pain spread out from the spot.

Oh, she was not good at this.

"There were some kids," Josh said. "But none that age group. There were two really little, and some young teens, but that's it." He shook his head in disgust. "Somebody tipped them off. Probably old Wiley himself."

Molly nodded noncommittally. "Well, if you hear anything about this little girl, let me know, will you?"

"She's probably two hundred miles away by now, Moll."

"You're right." Glad to have that done, she changed the subject. "So, how do you like that new truck?"

She called her doctor at home from a pay phone at the grocery store. "Hi, Dr. Harris," she said. "I have that sore throat again. Would you phone in a prescription for me?"

"Nasty infection, isn't it? My wife couldn't kick it for weeks, either." He agreed to phone it into the pharmacy at Judson's right away.

The pharmacist was solicitous when he filled the scrip, and again Molly felt a little guilty. But not too guilty. Her patient would be in trouble without the antibiotics, and the consequences of letting him go to the

authorities was higher than he ought to pay. A white
lie. Just a small one.

Still, it bothered her. People trusted her.

There wasn't anything else she could do tonight to
find the mysterious Josefina, and she took the bottle of
pills back home.

It had grown dark, and as she drove toward the house
on the narrow, two-lane blacktop that wound toward
her land, she instinctively slowed down. At a particularly nasty curve, she passed the *descanso,* a white
painted cross and wreath that marked the spot where
Willie Chacon had died in his '62 Buick seven years
ago, and slowed down again.

Her driveway was not paved. It cut through uncul-
tivated fields thick with sage, the gravel holding up,
but the red clay beneath it beginning to waffle and pot-
hole.

Looking at the wide bowl of black sky, at the depth
of the darkness, she wondered about the little girl,
where she was, what she was doing tonight. It broke
her heart to imagine how terrified an eight-year-old
would be on such a dark night. "Keep her safe," she
prayed silently, turning off the engine of her car.

The house looked exactly the same as it had when
she left it. A lamp burned in the back room where she'd
left her patient, and the light cast a faint wash of gold
over the spirea bushes at the side of the house. A ripple
of nervousness, of the vastness of her actions, suddenly
struck her, and she sat where she was, a little stunned
with it.

Was she nuts? Taking a stranger, however wounded,
into her home, with no protection to speak of, isolated
out here on her one hundred acres where no one could
hear her scream if he turned out to be a mass murderer?

For one moment, the fanciful side of her imagination conjured up a gory picture of herself slaughtered in her bed, a statistic for the ten o'clock news. On the screen of her mind, a grave-faced anchorman said somberly, "In other news tonight, a young woman was found murdered in a small town in northern New Mexico this morning...."

She heard her late husband snort in laughter, a memory, but one that brought her back to earth. He'd found her wild imagination both endearing and exasperating, and that gentle snort had always helped her reassert her practical side.

As it did now. Even if her patient were of that ilk, tonight he couldn't walk, much less chop her to pieces. She knew from her days as a surgical nurse that it wasn't as easy as it looked to wield a knife. It took quite a lot of strength, actually.

And besides all that, her bedroom door locked.

Chuckling to herself, she went in and checked on the man. One hand was flung out, and the covers had tangled around him, as if he'd been restless, but he still lay flat on his back, that black-licorice hair scattered over the pillowcase.

At his feet, curled in a big ball of fluffy black and white fur, was Leonardo, who had evidently decided the stranger was safe enough. Molly chuckled again, scrubbing his head lightly. "Taking good care of him?"

The cat purred, then yawned and jumped down, off to find food. Molly turned her attention to her patient, reaching down to tug the blanket over a long brown leg that had come uncovered. It was lean and dark and muscular, lightly adorned with black hair that looked silky, and to her amazement, Molly found the sight positively electrifying.

A leg, Moll, a wry voice said. *Just a leg.* With a sigh of exasperation at herself, she poured a glass of water, then squatted beside the bed to wake him. Only then did she realize she didn't know his name. How odd.

"*Señor,*" she said quietly, touching his forearm.

He didn't stir in the slightest. She shook his shoulder lightly. "*Señor,*" she said again, more loudly this time. Still nothing.

Suddenly worried, Molly put her hand on his face and swore at the fever burning in him. "Damn." Not good. Not good at all.

Putting the water down on the table, she raced to the kitchen for a clean washcloth and pot of water into which she cracked a tray of ice cubes. Carrying those supplies, she dashed into the bathroom for a bottle of rubbing alcohol and back into the bedroom.

Her heart was racing with fear, and pouring liberal amounts of sharp-smelling isopropyl alcohol onto the cloth, she tried again to rouse him. "*Señor,* wake up!" She tossed the covers off his body and washed his face, his neck, his arms. "*Señor!* Can you hear me?"

He stirred a little, and Molly redoubled her efforts. The scissors she'd used earlier on his jeans now lay on the table and she grabbed them, quickly slicing away the thin tank top he wore. She spilled fresh alcohol on the cloth and washed his chest methodically. "*Señor!*" she cried, then more quietly, "Come on, guy. If you die on me, I'm in really big trouble."

The voice came from far, far away. Soft, like music, like morning. Alejandro reached for it, but it slid away, and he was back home, on his uncle's farm. Confused but pleased, he greeted his cousins and explained that he didn't know how he'd got here, but he was glad. Then one asked about Josefina.

Josefina!

A sharp splat hit his forehead, and he bolted upward, fighting. A strong arm caught him midchest and pushed him back down, and roaring pain jolted through his ribs and from his leg, simultaneously, and he groaned, falling back, dizzy and nauseated.

"Take it easy," a woman's voice said. "I'm just trying to bring down your fever, okay? Easy."

The cold cloth fell on his neck, and he protested, or thought he did. It came again, across his chest, his shoulders. Finally, the sharp odor penetrated and he found himself beginning to shiver. Protesting, he opened his eyes.

His saint bent over him, worry on her face now as she patiently washed his flesh down, rubbing his chest, his neck, his face, then his shoulders and arms, then each leg, and back to his chest. Lost just beyond the ability to speak, he only watched her. The braid, glossy and long, fell over her shoulder as she worked, and he noticed that her nose was very straight and a little too big for her face. And he saw that her eyes were strange—tilted down a little at the inner corners. It made her seem otherworldly.

At last she seemed to feel his gaze and jerked her head up. There was deep worry in the gray eyes before relief claimed it. She sighed. "Thank God," she whispered. "*Señor,*" she said, "I must give you a pill. Can you take it with my help?"

He could not quite recall how to speak, but he made some motion she must have taken for yes, because one strong arm came behind his shoulders, bracing him. A breast, giving and warm, pushed into his shoulder. A pill landed in his mouth. It was slippery on his tongue. She put a glass to his mouth and he drank. Then another pill. More water.

Water. He closed his eyes. In his disoriented state, he thought of it as cool silver, thought of it rushing over the orange fire in his throat. Then the glass was gone. He drifted away. Josefina came to his thoughts again. He had to get well. To find her.

Molly was afraid to leave him. Washing him with alcohol brought the fever down some, and in time the ibuprofen and antibiotics would begin to work their magic. In the meantime, he was obviously delirious and restless, his fingers sometimes fluttering up as if to capture something just out of reach, his head turning side to side in blind seeking.

Her belly went hollow as she examined him, finding the wound red and inflamed, his skin dry and hot, even after the rubdown. She would have to remain vigilant until his fever broke. In a few hours, she would awaken him again, give him some more ibuprofen and antibiotics and water, and pray he could keep them down. It had been at least a full day since he'd eaten, probably closer to twenty-four hours, and the meds might not sit well.

He moaned and threw back the covers. Patiently, Molly replaced them and then went to the kitchen to boil water for tea. She made a huge mug of sweetened black tea with milk, then found the novel she was reading and settled in the small back room.

In the silence of the desert night, in the quiet of her own house, Molly told herself she ought to be worried. If her patient died, she'd have an awful lot of explaining to do. The people she'd lied to this evening would know she'd lied, and they would not trust her again so quickly.

But he would not die. She wouldn't let him. He might be pretty miserable by morning. He might curse her before she was through with him. But he wasn't going to die.

As she sat in the cozy "mama" chair she'd purchased in hopes of having a baby that had never come, it wasn't worry in her mind. Now that the crisis was passed, she felt…anticipation.

Anticipation for what?

Did it matter? No. She granted herself permission to admire the blackness of his hair and realized she would very much like to put her hands into it. She eyed the length of a shin sticking out of the covers and liked the silky-looking hair glazing his coppery-colored skin, liked the strength in that calf. She liked his foot, graceful and clean, and the oval silver saint's medal glinting on his chest and the long swoop of collarbone.

But over and over, she came back to his face. It was not traditionally or even classically handsome; the shape was long and narrow, wider at the top than the bottom. Taken one by one, the angles were too sharp— a blade of a nose jutting aggressively from between high, piercingly slanted cheekbones. An authoritative jaw leading to a narrow chin.

She sipped her tea and inclined her head. Painting was her hobby, and line had become something of a fascination for her. Why did all those sharp angles work? His face was drawn like a coyote's, almost too severe and lean. And yet, the effect was undeniably riveting. Why?

The lines balanced, slant to slant, in perfect harmony. His skin was clear and dark, blunting the shadows. And there was balance to the severity, in the softness of lashes and eyebrows, in the wide mouth graced with lips that were drawn extravagantly, almost lushly.

And around that sharply etched face fell hair as black as a silk scarf, loose and curling in places, a tendril breaking that bold cheekbone, another curling along his neck.

She closed her eyes, aware of a vague heat along her inner thighs. *Stop.*

But why? How long since she'd felt this quivering thrill at even looking at a man? Forever. And ever. There had not been a man in her life in four years, and for six before that, her husband had occupied—and satisfied—all of her fantasies.

That was all she indulged tonight: the simple pleasure of finally feeling a stir in those places she'd thought dead with her husband.

A fantasy, that was all.

She had no illusions about the reality of the world. He was an illegal immigrant—which meant poor and even more poorly educated. He would know nothing of the things that she loved—her books and poetry and music and art. She would not deny the native intelligence she had glimpsed in his eyes, but she didn't confuse education with knowledge. She didn't confuse beauty with goodness, either.

But the fantasy, now…the fantasy was quite different. It did not involve anything but direct physicality. Alone in her chair, with no one to see her, she could admit to herself that it would be very pleasant, very *very* pleasant to lie naked against that long, lean body, lie with him and touch him and feel his hands and mouth on her. She would like it very much.

But they would never have a thing in common. In a few days, he would be well enough to walk, and he would take his Josefina and wander to the next town, to the next harvest, the next dodge of the law.

In the meantime, he quieted, and Molly let herself simply look at him, resting her eyes on his beauty in much the way she would gaze at a sunrise. Peacefully, without demand.

At last, she opened her book. Propping her feet on the end of the bed, and covering her shoulders with the blue and green crocheted afghan she'd made the first year in the house, she read. Leonardo wandered in, jumped up on her lap for a nice rubdown, and having achieved it, leaped from her lap to the bed, curling at the stranger's side and settling in to lick a paw.

Molly thought about shooing him away, but it somehow made her feel better that the skittish Leo had decided the stranger was okay. She went back to reading, and after a little while, she dozed, then fell into a much deeper sleep, her head comfortable against the back of the chair.

Something startled her awake, and she dropped her book, blinking in disorientation when she found herself in the chair. In a rush she remembered her patient, and saw that it was he who had awakened her.

He was struggling to sit up, and had reached out a hand to touch her leg. "*Señora,*" he said in a rough voice, "I am sorry but..."

Immediately, Molly bolted forward, putting her hands on his cheeks to test his fever. She found the skin damp and hot. Damn. "Let me help. What do you need?"

He looked abashed, and raised a hand to gesture toward the room across the hall, where the light still burned. "I cannot get up."

"Oh! Excellent." She patted his shoulder gently. "Let me get a bedpan. Don't move." She rushed out of the room and found an old tin pot that would serve the purpose, and mindful of his privacy, held it out to him, ready to turn her back when he took it.

"No, no," he protested, and pushed himself up. "Help me."

"It's all right. I'm a nurse." She didn't really know how much he understood of her English. He seemed to be quite fluent and until he proved otherwise, she'd stick to her usual conversational style. "You don't have to get up."

A dark flush crossed his cheekbones, and he looked away. "No." With what appeared to be Herculean effort, he managed to swing his legs over the bed and sit up. "Please." He held out a hand to her. "Help me."

Molly nodded and bent down to allow him to put his arm around her shoulder. Together they rose, and the bedspread fell away, leaving him in clean white briefs, nothing fancy and somehow all the sexier for it. Rotten of her, she thought with a half smile, to be admiring the fit of a patient's underwear. Sensing he might be embarrassed, she tugged the afghan from the chair and with one hand, wrapped it around his waist. With his free hand, he captured the ends to hold it in place, and Molly lifted her head to smile at him.

He looked at her gravely, and she saw that his eyes were very large and dark and liquid—*limpid*. The word sounded in her mind, a poet's description. His mouth was tight, and a paleness marked the flesh around it, but he managed a faint twitch that might have been a smile. "Thank you."

"De nada." She helped him across the hallway and he grabbed the door, bracing himself on the sink with arms that trembled visibly. "Are you sure you're okay?"

He stood there, head bent. Light melted along the tense muscles of his back, showing the effort it took for him to stand there. After a moment, he nodded, and she reached for the door to close it for him. "I'll be right here. Cry out if you need me."

Leaning on the wall outside, she wondered again if she'd lost her mind. As if he wondered, too, Leonardo peeked around the edge of the wall, alarm on his face.

The woman, tousled, and weary by the look of her face, helped him back to his bed and tucked the blankets around him. He had been overheated and now felt very cold. Was that good? He thought so.

"Can you eat a little?" she asked him.

He could. His stomach felt as empty as a dry arroyo, but she had been kind enough already. "Go back to sleep. Morning is soon enough."

Her smile was quick and friendly. Alejandro liked the way her eyes crinkled with it. "I'd much rather you ate, so I can give you some more medicine. Just a little broth or something?"

"Broth?"

"Soup. *¿Sopa?*"

And though he knew he should not accept more of her kindness, his stomach ached for something. "Yes, please."

"Bueno."

He smiled at her attempts at his native language. Like most gringos, she flattened it with her American accent, but it was kind of her to make the attempt. She

bustled out and Alejandro lay back on the pillows, pulling the blankets more tightly around himself and closing his eyes.

He'd tossed Josefina bodily into a copse of bushes
and taken off himself into the darkness, bolting like a
wolf, away from the raid. He'd believed he'd made it,
too, until the bullet caught him. Even then, he kept
running as long as he could, determined he would not
leave Josefina to the authorities as long as he had
breath in his body.

But even a shallow bullet wound was enough to
make him bleed too much, and the running made it
worse, and he was weak and stumbling by the time
he'd thought to pack dirt and grass into it. He'd taken
a few minutes to clear his head, listen in the darkness
to the faint sounds of the raid. Intending to circle back
toward the lights and the place he'd hidden Josefina,
he got to his feet and leaned into a small run.

In the darkness and his confusion, he made a wrong
step and found himself suddenly hurtling through the
darkness. Not a long fall, but it had not been easy on
the way down. And the wind had slammed out of him,
harsh and shattering. And he had not been able to get
back up, no matter how the screams of Josefina echoed
in his head.

Josefina. It made him sick to think of her alone tonight.

The woman came back with a tray she set on the
bedside table. As she bent, the soft lamplight caught
on strands of her hair, turning them to a silver-gilt
shade that disappeared again when she straightened.
"Here we go," she said.

There was a bowl of thin soup and a glass of milk
and a cloth napkin. "Do you need help?"

He shook his head, but she did help him to sit up properly, putting piles of pillows behind his back so he could lean against the wall. The tray had little legs that fit over his lap. But now, shirtless, he was cold, and rubbed his arm. "Where is my shirt?"

"Oh! I had to cut it off. Your jeans, too, I'm afraid." She turned, as if looking for the shirt, and he thought she was more unsettled than she appeared at first. "Let me get you one."

She left and came back with a denim shirt with pockets. A man's shirt. Was she married? "Your husband's?" he asked as she helped him put it on.

"Yeah," she said shortly.

"He will not mind?"

Her smile was sad. "No."

So he was gone. He nodded and picked up his spoon and began to eat. It was exactly what he wanted. Not too much, but enough to take the hollowness out of him. He thought of her attempt at Spanish and said, "This...broth? We call it *caldo.*"

"Ah, *caldo,*" she repeated "Not *sopa.*"

"Soup and *sopa,* broth and *caldo.*"

"I see." She linked her hands around her knee and smiled. He liked that smile, very much, and he smiled in return.

A flicker crossed her face—something startled—and to hide it, she ducked her head for a moment. "Do you mind if I ask your name?"

"I am Alejandro Sosa," he said. "And I am in your debt, *señora.*"

"No. The angels put you where I'd find you," she added with another smile. "So they must have meant for me to fix you up."

He bowed his head, humbled. "I will repay you,"

he said with as much dignity as he could muster in his weakened state. He wished that he had his hair combed and his jaw shaved, so that he looked less like the field-worker she had found and more like the son of his father. "Whatever you ask."

"Don't worry about it," she said casually. "How is your stomach? Upset?"

"No."

"Good. Then I want to—"

"Not *bueno?*" he said lightly.

It snared her, that little question and littler smile. Her face, very businesslike, shifted again and she lifted her eyes to his, *seeing* him. And he saw her. The fine bones of her face, the clearness of pale, pale eyes, the wisps of hair loose around her jaw and neck. *Huera,* they would call her where he came from, and say it in a soft voice of esteem. And he noticed that her body was not large, as he'd come to think. She was tall but narrow-shouldered, wide through the hips and small through the chest. Very strong.

She swallowed, looked away. "I'm sorry, Señor Sosa. I didn't mean to be patronizing."

Regret touched him. "Oh, no. It was a joke, *señora.*" He made a wry face. "A bad one, eh?"

That drew a chuckle. "No. Just small."

She took the tray and put the milk in his hand, then gave him a handful of pills. "You will feel much better by morning," she promised.

"Bueno," he said, and took them.

She smiled. "Good night, Mr. Sosa."

"Wait!"

At the door already, she turned.

"I do not know your name, *señora.* The saint who rescued me."

"You can call me Saint Molly."

Molly. Satisfied, he settled back down, wincing at the pain in his ribs, and closed his eyes. Just before he fell asleep, he realized he had forgotten to ask about Josefina.

Chapter 3

Josh couldn't sleep. He slid out of bed, careful not to wake his sleeping wife, and put on his robe, padding into the kitchen to get a drink of water. The buzz of the neon light overhead was the only noise, and somehow the silence exaggerated the noise of the raid, in his mind.

The raid last night was what kept him awake. They'd been planning it for a week, timing it to hurt Wiley as much as possible, so that maybe he'd finally recognize he couldn't keep hiring illegals to work his land. Not that it did any good. Next week, there would be a whole new crew. But they raided him regularly anyway. It was so routine as to be boring.

But last night, things had been off from the beginning. For one thing, there had been a lot more migrants than they'd anticipated, and there were more women and youths with them than usual, which always complicated matters. The deputies had also surprised them in the middle of a party, and the younger men were inclined to argue and resist, creating a tense and panicked environment. One young man had panicked and punched an officer, which led to complete chaos. Workers had scattered in every direction, with officers chasing them into the dark fields and the vast peach orchard at the western end of the farms.

And that was when things went crazy. Josh kept seeing it, over and over, in his mind. Lifting his weapon, firing. Once, twice, the gun making a light in the darkness. He heard the man fall, and ran after him, but although he'd walked back and forth, side to side, for well over an hour, Josh had never found him.

It made Josh sick. He'd not breathed a word of it to anyone. No one had said a word to him, either, although someone must have heard the shots. It wasn't the first time. Technically, they weren't supposed to use their weapons in such raids unless they were in physical danger. Realistically, the job was so frustrating, it had happened many times.

Until now, Josh had been a model deputy, but lately, as he struggled with his bills—particularly the high price of medical insurance for his family—his resentment grew. He bought groceries with hard-earned cash, and burned when someone presented food stamps. He was furious that the county was paying hundreds of thousands of dollars a year to cover the costs of the illegal immigrants in town from March to October, jail costs, housing costs, welfare and medical care, when the same county could barely afford his subsistence-level salary.

He was barely surviving. Some months it was a choice between paying twenty on the electric bill or letting the long-distance portion of his phone get cut off. His new truck was a ten-year-old model that he'd had to have to get around this winter.

He just didn't understand why he had to suffer, and yet hundreds and hundreds of people who weren't even citizens got taken care of. It wasn't fair.

But it had been wrong to let his sense of outrage infect his job. He winced again, remembering. God, he hoped he hadn't killed anyone.

Molly moved quietly around the house the next morning. She had not awakened at her usual 5:00 a.m., but slept in until six-thirty, and light was pouring through the kitchen windows, splashing into the sink and across the terra-cotta counters and glazing the fashionably distressed cabinets. She'd done all the work herself, and the room was her favorite.

The house, built in the twenties, had come with the land, which was about the only good thing Molly could have said about it those first few years. Not a single thing in it had been changed or updated in the intervening decades, and her husband had tackled each room one by one.

Most of his time had been spent between his regular carpentry job and on the land itself, which had been his passion, so the interior work had gone slowly. When he was killed by a lightning strike, the kitchen had still been a nightmare—tin cabinets covered with peeling pine-style Contact paper, peeling linoleum, a stove with only two working burners.

A few weeks after Tim was buried, the stove had caught fire. The resulting smoke damage and need for a working stove had been a blessing in disguise. Night after sleepless night, weekend after lonely weekend,

Molly had expended her grief and loneliness on the kitchen.

As she measured coffee into the automatic coffee-maker, she admired the baskets lined up on top of the cupboards, the African violets blooming in the wide greenhouse window and the display of her herb and rose gardens beyond—the project she'd taken up after the kitchen.

She needed a new project, she supposed. Heaven knew, there was always something waiting in a house this old.

Finally, having delayed long enough, she tiptoed down the short hall to the back bedroom and peeked in on her patient. Morning sunlight poured through the row of white eyelet curtains, and onto the man still asleep in the small double bed.

She'd been hoping he might be a little less... overwhelming by daylight. No such luck. She paused in the doorway, admiring the smooth copper angle of his elbow, the breadth of his wrists and the fine, large hand cast loosely over his waist. Nearby the pillow, Leo was curled comfortably, his tail covering his eyes.

As if her gaze awakened him, the man stirred, legs shifting below the blankets until the remembrance of pain in one of them stopped him. He went still again, and only turned his head, shaking hair from his face. He opened his eyes.

Molly felt a hitch in her throat. Stunning eyes, star-tlingly dark irises against whites as clear as a child's. For a moment, he stared at her, perplexed, then lifted that big dark hand and brushed his hair all the way out of his face. "I thought I dreamed you," he said.

Oh, my. His voice, till now, had been rough with

pain, his words broken. After sleep and antibiotics, the voice was as rich as Mexican coffee, the accent lacing through it like cinnamon, a delicious and surprising stroke. "I'm real," she said, crossing her arms. "How are you feeling?"

He inclined his head, as if listening to his body. "Not bad."

She smiled. "Not bad, or just better than yesterday?"

He raised his eyebrows, a faint smile of agreement turning up his wide mouth. "Not great."

"I'm going to make some scrambled eggs for breakfast. And there's coffee. Can you eat?"

"Oh, yes." It was heartfelt.

Abruptly, he sat up and Molly flew to his side when the stabbing pain of broken ribs made him put both hands to his chest with a strangled groan. His hair fell in his face. "Take it easy," she said.

Leonardo, disturbed, made a plaintive noise of complaint and sat up by the pillows, but he didn't run this time. Interesting, Molly thought.

The man's breath stuttered, then settled, and he raised his head. "Did you find my niece?"

"Not yet."

Despair flickered over his face and he closed his eyes. "I have to find her."

"*Señor,* you are not able. Don't worry—I haven't stopped looking." She put a hand on his arm. "Let me get us both some breakfast, and give you some more medicine, and I'm going over to the orchard to see if Wiley has found her."

"Wiley." He nodded very seriously, put a hand on her shoulder, patting. "Yeah. That's good."

"Need some help up?"

"Sí." He said it with resignation, and Molly chuckled.

"You'll be better in just a day or two, I promise."

He nodded. "I do not like this—" his dark hand swept out, as if to fling the weakness away "—fault."

"I know." With practiced gestures, she indicated he should put his arm around her shoulders and they stood up together. She glanced up to his face, and saw his jaw set very tightly, that licorice hair hiding everything else. The pain had to be intense, but he bore it fairly well.

She helped him limp across the hall, and left him, pointing out towels and soap and a plastic, wrapped toothbrush she'd put on the sink, before leaving him to it. "Call me when you're ready, and I'll help you get to the kitchen," she said. He gave a single nod.

Molly went back to the kitchen and without thought, she turned on the radio, and poured a cup of coffee and turned to the fridge, opened the door and stared for a long time without seeing anything but the fall of his hair, his bladed face, the red-gold burnishing of his skin.

Slowly the vision faded, leaving her staring blankly at the contents of her refrigerator. Eggs. Right. She took the carton out, grabbed the butter, closed the door.

From around the corner came Leonardo, with that air of a busy tiger, a prize in his mouth. Molly smiled. "Found a sock, did you?" He adored socks for reasons Molly couldn't fathom. He stole them from the laundry pile and the bathroom and bedroom floors, where she all too often left them, and carried them proudly to a corner of the dining room. He hustled now to that stash, where one green one and one pink-flowered one waited. The significance of the fact that the one he added now was white—and therefore belonged to Alejandro, sunk in. "Oh no you don't. Wait a minute, Leo."

"Señora?"

Deciding she could rescue the sock later, Molly rushed back down the hall. "Yes?"

"I need...um...pants?"

"Oh!" Her eyes slid to the opening in the door, thinking of the silky hair on his thighs—

Startled by the vividly erotic memory, she blinked. "Of course you do. I'll be right back."

Pants. Hauling open a drawer in the heavy Spanish colonial pine bureau, she riffled through a stack of clothes that she'd been unable to bear getting rid of. "Ah-ha!" She grabbed a pair of drawstring gray sweats and hurried back. "Here you are," she said.

He stuck a hand out of the door, his face at the opening. *"Gracias."*

"I'll wait this time."

In a moment, he opened the door and, holding on to the jamb, his shoulders hunched, he mugged an old man's voice and posture, his feet shuffling. *"El viejo* needs you."

Molly laughed and settled his arm over her shoulder and tried not to notice the feeling of his body close to hers. He smelled of soap and peppermint toothpaste, a somehow intimate scent.

At the doorway of the kitchen, he paused, lifting his head, his free hand still clasped to his chest. "Oh, very nice."

"Thanks," she said briskly and deposited him in a chair. "Coffee?"

"Yes, please."

"Anything to put in it? Milk? Sugar?"

He waved a hand as she settled a mug in front of him. "Everything."

Conscious of his frank gaze, Molly grabbed the sugar, then opened the fridge again for the milk, feeling a little heat in her cheeks as she thought of herself mooning over the eggs a few minutes ago. How embarrassing—she was acting as if she'd never looked at a man before.

But no matter how she tried to keep her body in a normal posture, move it in the ways she'd moved it a thousand billion times over the thirty years of her life, it was impossible. She was aware of her fingers around the neck of the milk carton, aware of the swing of her arm as she took it out, aware of her knees moving her across the buff-colored ceramic tiles she'd laid herself, on those very knees. She was aware, especially, of her breasts beneath her T-shirt, and of her rear end when she turned around to start cooking breakfast.

And worse, it was nothing he did to make her so aware. He did not stare inappropriately. His gaze did not particularly linger on her. He was polite and graceful, and openly looking around himself to see where he'd landed.

It was just him. Having a man in her kitchen after so long, a man unrelated to her.

"*Señora,* may I ask what you learned about Josefina?"

The formality of his words, the dignity in his question brought her to earth. With relief, she seized the sense of normality and broke eggs into a bowl, turning on the burner at the same time to heat the cast-iron skillet. "Very little, I'm afraid. I asked a sheriff if any children had been taken in the raid, and there were no girls her age. So she's out there, somewhere."

"Thank you." He bowed his head.

Beating eggs with a fork, she said, "How did you come to leave her behind?"

He took a breath, blew it out. "She cannot run so fast. I hid her." He met her gaze. "I have no visa, no green card."

Molly smiled. "I gathered that."

He nodded, the dark eyes troubled. "This could make trouble for you."

She lifted a shoulder. "I know that, too."

"So why did you help me, *señora?*"

"I couldn't leave you there." Turning, she put butter in the pan. "No, that's not true. I was going to call an ambulance, but you started calling for Josefina." She looked over her shoulder, and met his gaze honestly. "I could tell you love her, and you were worried."

He swallowed. Nodded.

She scrambled the eggs briskly, poured them onto two plates and carried them to the table. "Anything else?"

"No, no." He frowned. "Please sit. This is very good."

From the corner of her eye, she noticed that he put his napkin in his lap, and sat with his back straight, and he held his fork correctly. No, more than correctly. Elegantly.

What had she expected? The answer shamed her. Not this. She had expected ignorance and sloppiness. A hand clutched around the midsection of a fork that shoveled the food into a mouth that chewed openly.

"Where are you from?" she asked.

"A place called Jaral, Mexico. Do you know it?"

"No." She smiled. "I'm afraid I don't."

He swept a lean-fingered hand. "It is very small. A long way from here."

"You must have been here a long time. Your English is very good."

"Not so long." He sipped some of the coffee. "When we were children, we lived in Mexico City. I had good schools. And when I came here, two years ago, I read the newspapers every day, to remember."

"Really?"

He straightened, putting his fork down. "You want to know why I am in those fields if what I say is true, no?"

Molly lifted her shoulders, let them go. "Yes."

He nodded. "I will tell you. Later. When you come back from Wiley."

She smiled. "Fair enough." Finished, she took her plate and gestured toward his. "Do you want something more to eat?"

There was strain around his mouth. "No. Thank you. *Viejo* goes back to bed." He attempted a smile, but it was plain that the simple business of washing and eating had drained him.

"Let's get you back to bed, then, *viejo*."

Josefina did not feel so good when she woke up. Her back hurt from the cold ground and her arms and legs were stiff from the long night without covers. The little dog had helped, but it was getting close now to winter, and in the cool bite of the morning, she could feel winter coming.

And her cough, usually no problem in the daytime, was bad this morning. It burned through her chest like the fingernails of a ghost, clawing at her. The inhaler didn't help, either. She coughed so hard she thought she was going to lose her stomach through her mouth. Finally the hacking stopped, and she leaned against the tree under which she'd slept, her eyes closed, just breathing, the way Tío showed her. In, out, very even, very slow, till all the feeling went away.

She wanted him to fix her tea with lemon and honey, so hot it almost burned her tongue. It would make her throat feel better. It would warm her tummy. It would—

Where *was* he? Where was everybody? These orchards and fields had been full, full for all the days they were here, and now they were completely empty. And the crop had not been brought in. Overhead, she could see the heavy fruit, almost too ripe, most of it. Her stomach growled.

She shimmied up the slender branches and nabbed a peach, so big it nearly didn't fit her hand, and then, not knowing if the dog would want to share with her, got another. He didn't want her fruit when she let him smell it, and so Josefina had two big peaches for breakfast. Later, when it got dark, she would go to town again, buy another hot dog for supper, maybe two— one for her and one for her dog.

Scratching the ragged mutt's soft ears, she said, "Everything is going to be okay, *pequeña.* You'll see." Meanwhile, it was nice not to be alone.

Molly drove under the Wiley Farms sign, waving as she passed a woman selling red wooden buckets of peaches, long green Anaheim and tiny, blisteringly hot habañero chiles. The farm offices were located farther in, in a building with a red roof painted with the orchard brand. "Hi, Joe," she said to the leather-faced foreman as she stepped out of her car. "Where's Wiley this morning?"

"How you doing, Molly?" He winked. "Ready to marry me yet?"

She smiled. "Maybe tomorrow."

He cocked his head toward the orchard. "He's back there. But beware—he's in a foul damned humor."

"Thanks." She headed toward the trees and shielded her eyes. "Hello, Wiley!" she called to a wiry man in a plaid shirt, jeans and boots. "You got a minute?"

"Always have time for a pretty lady." He jumped down from the seat of a tractor. "What can I do for you?"

Molly glanced over her shoulder. Three other men, obviously working on the engine, looked at them curiously. "Let's walk a minute," she said.

He allowed himself to be led to a spot beneath a plucked-clean tree. "What's up, Moll? Is there a problem?"

"There is, actually," she said. "I'm looking for a little girl. Her name is Josefina, and she was with one of your migrant workers during the raid. But—" she bit her lip, stuck her hands in her back pockets "—she's missing now."

He pursed his lips. "I'd like to help you, honey, but there's nobody here. Whoever was left after the raid were gone by morning. I got about twenty guys working the chile fields, but they're all from the valley."

Molly sighed. "Do you remember her? About eight?" She realized she still had no clear description. "There couldn't have been too many girls her age."

He frowned. "You know, there was a tyke about that age. Had a bad cough, and I sent her and her uncle

over to Health Services to have it looked at. He got
nabbed in the raid.''

Her uncle. Bingo.

For a minute, Molly hesitated, unsure whether to
trust him with the whole story. This lying business
wasn't as easy as it looked on television.

But in the end, she chose to err on the side of caution, and repeated the myth she'd generated for her
brother. ''I don't know about the uncle, but she used
to come see me in the garden.'' She pointed in the
direction of her land. ''I've been worried about her,
and asked my brother if they got her, but they didn't.''
She closed her eyes, no longer faking it. ''It's been a
full twenty-four hours. Will you keep an eye out for
her? Maybe send someone around to check the fields?''

''It won't hurt anything to look around, I guess. Poor
kid.'' His blue eyes sharpened. ''As I recall, that uncle
of hers was a real good-lookin' fella. Sure it's not him
you're worried about?''

Molly bowed her head before she realized it looked
like an admission of guilt. On the spur of the moment,
she said, ''Well, I might have seen him once or twice.''
With an abashed smile, she lifted her eyebrows. ''Not
my type. It's Josefina I'm worried about.''

''I'll keep an eye out, honey.'' He frowned, concerned now. ''Don't you be mixing with these guys,
now. I know it gets real lonely, you being a widow and
all, but some of these fellas are downright mean and
ain't got a thing to lose.''

She smiled. ''Not to worry.'' She lifted a hand.
''Thanks, Wiley.''

''You might distract that bulldog brother of yours
the next day or two.'' He made a grimace. ''I got a
truckload of new guys coming in and I don't need no

more trouble. Most of 'em got their visas this time, but I need every hand I can get. The chiles got to come in before the first freeze.'' He looked at the sky. "Likely to be any day now.''

And the little girl was still out there. Molly nodded. "I'll see what I can do.''

Alejandro slept for a long time. He didn't know exactly how long, but when he stirred, the bright sunlight had gone from the room. It was very quiet in the house, so his saint had not yet returned.

A black-and-white cat sat on the windowsill, his long tail swishing as he eyed something outside. With a fond smile, Alejandro lifted a hand and brushed his fingers over the curve of tail. *"Hola, gato.''*

The cat looked down with round yellow eyes, the alertness showing his youth. Alejandro shifted enough to put his hand under the blanket and wiggled his fingers. The cat's eyes widened and he pounced, a purr roaring out from him as he chased the fingers from one place to another under the blanket.

Lying there, Alejandro grew aware of the extraordinary luxury he found himself in. The bed was comfortable, big enough for his long legs. The room was clean and warm, and he could not remember the last time he'd had the pleasure of awakening to the company of a house cat. But most profound was the silence. In the migrant camps, there was always noise. Noise of other people, noise of machines and radios. It was not something he noticed ordinarily, but with the silence as comparison, he was amazed to discover how much he'd missed it.

This was what Josefina needed. Peace and quiet and a normal life. With a pet to sleep with her and school every morning. It made him ache a little to realize she probably didn't even remember such a life.

The thought of Josefina compelled him to move. While Molly was gone, he had a good chance to see what he could do on his own. Slowly, he got out of bed, and hanging on to walls and chairs, made his way toward the kitchen. The leg hurt, but he could keep his weight more or less on the other one. It was his chest that killed him. Everything made it hurt.

Going very slowly, he made it to the kitchen. It took an age to take a glass from the cupboard, another year to move three feet to the sink and turn on the faucet. Lifting his arm to his mouth with the full glass hurt a lot more than it had this morning.

Sweating, he leaned on the counter, despising the weakness that made his arms tremble, made him faintly dizzy. Just walking. Just drinking. He already wanted to go back to bed.

Instead, he forced himself to move to the long glass doors that led to the garden. The sun drew him and he stood in its light, not daring to step outside where someone might see him. Even blunted by the glass, the warmth of the rays felt good to him. He imagined he could feel the long fingers moving into his ribs, knitting them back together, imagined them putting healing palms against the wound in his thigh.

It helped. For a moment. Then he found himself gritting his teeth to stay standing so straight. Felt the sweat of effort trickling down his back.

With longing, he thought of a bath. He'd managed to wash his face and torso this morning, but his hair stuck to his head and he could feel the remnants of his feverish sleep down his back. He did not mind being honestly dirty, when he was sweaty from a day in the sun, or dusty from horses or the fields. But he did not like this. And without the woman's help, he did not see how he could bathe, but he also disliked being so dependent upon her.

He wiped his face wearily. His mind felt dull, formless. Until his brain cleared, he could not imagine the next steps he would have to take. For a moment, he bowed his head, feeling defeated.

Ah, Josefina! *Hija!*

He had let her down, and could not think how to find her, what do to. He was not a man who relied on others. He took pride in his ability to manage his life and his world, whatever that entailed, but this went beyond his experiences. He did not fall to illness or weakness. He'd once worked an entire day with a broken wrist and never minded it.

Gritting his teeth, he raised his head. This would not defeat him, either. His gaze caught on the machine that had made coffee this morning. Coffee might clear his head. Would the woman mind? He thought of her solicitousness and thought she would not. He moved, plodding but sure, to examine it. There was a button to turn it on, but he did not see where to put the water. Or the coffee. He glared at it.

But he could make coffee another way. He remembered seeing her put the can in the cupboard by the stove. He put it on the counter, and then, biting his lip as he reached, moved things around. Brown sugar. Cinnamon. At first he was disappointed, only finding the ground kind, but he moved a box of cornstarch and spied a glass bottle of stick cinnamon.

Excellent.

It had taken him a solid five minutes to do that much, but the act made him feel stronger. From beneath the counter, he took a saucepan and limped to the sink to measure water into it. The next step was more difficult—carrying the water to the stove without spilling it. He splashed a few drops over the edge of the pan, but managed to get it to the stove and turn it on.

Then he settled on a stool close by the stove and waited for the boiling, for the steps that would make coffee the way he needed it this morning. He gazed out the window and hoped his saint would come back in time to share a little with him. He hoped she would bring news of Josefina.

Staring out at the blue and dun landscape, he imagined he could see her, his bright, smart niece. He chose to imagine her in a sunny place, calm and thoughtful. A little lonely, but not afraid. He willed her to remember all the things they had practiced for just such an emergency, and he suddenly realized what a foolish, foolish chance he had taken.

It had to end. It was becoming too dangerous, and would grow worse as she took on the contours of a woman's body—and not only when there were raids. The camps were full of young men, away from their homes and the people who knew them. They were lonely. Josefina would tempt them—and then there would be real trouble.

With a breathy exclamation, he shook his head. This was no life for a child. No life for him. He ached with homesickness, ached to go back to the simple farmer's life he'd known before his sister's death. And yet, when he spoke to his uncle rarely, it was plain that life in Mexico was no better. The big farms were eating up the little ones, making it harder and harder to make a living from the land. And there were so many people displaced from that land now that the cities were overcrowded, wages were poor, the neighborhoods where a man could afford to house a family too dangerous. Though everyone said it was different in America, he saw some of the same things here. It was just easier to be poor with three dollars an hour, rather than the three dollars a day he could get for the same work at home.

He did not know what the answer was. It weighed on him every day, thinking of it.

His head ached with the questions, and he put them aside for today. Today, he had to let himself heal. Today, he hoped to find Josefina. When she was found, then he could decide what to do.

Chapter 4

Molly made a few more stops before she returned home, avoiding her usual haunts in hopes of sidestepping anyone who'd ask about her "sore throat." She was lucky. The market was not busy, and she nabbed a few items to tide them over till morning, then got to her car without having to speak to hardly anyone.

When she unlocked the door at her house, an aroma of freshly brewed coffee filled her nose, so rich it made her nearly light-headed. Carrying the bag of groceries into the kitchen, she made a show of inhaling deeply.

"Oh, I must need that coffee! It smells glorious."

Her patient sat on a kitchen stool by the stove, one hand stirring a pot, the other clasped protectively around his ribs. He lifted his head. "I hoped you would not mind me taking this liberty, if the coffee was good enough."

"Not at all. As it happens, I had a yen for some doughnuts, so I stopped at the store." She brought out a bag of tender, newly fried doughnuts. "Do you like them?"

"Yes, I do." He attempted a smile, and only then did Molly see the white lines of strain around his mouth, the faint sheen of sweat on his forehead. "The coffee will be ready in—" he glanced at the clock "—three minutes."

Concerned, she crossed the room and with the familiarity of a nurse to her patient, touched his shoulder, bending to look into his eyes. "Are you all right?"

He ignored her. "Did you find her?"

Molly sighed. Shook her head. "Wiley is going to keep an eye out. He said he'll send some men to look for her." Automatically, she put her hand on his face to check for fever.

She regretted it immediately. Her thumb against his cheekbone was very white, very alien, did not belong anywhere near him. And beneath her fingertips, she felt a delicacy and strength of bone that was powerfully intimate. His eyes, sober and large and still, regarded her steadily.

She took her hand away. "The fever is back a little. You should have some more medicine and go back to bed."

"In a little while. First coffee, huh?" He lifted his chin to the bag on the counter. "And a doughnut or two." A faint smile edged the wide mouth. "Or three."

"Ah, so you're like me—a weakness for doughnuts."

"My mother cooked them. I think of her."

From the cupboard behind her, Molly took two mugs and set them on the counter. "I've never seen coffee made this way."

"You will like it." Very carefully, he stood up. "I

need a…'' He scowled, his hand describing a shape in the air. "You know, something to pour it through."

"Ah." She ducked below the cabinet and pulled out a large wire-mesh strainer. "This?"

"*Sí.*"

"Strainer," she said.

He gave a single nod, took it from her and pointed to the stove. "It is too heavy to lift now." His wry smile. "Will you do it?"

Together they strained the coffee into the cups. The scented aroma made Molly's mouth water. "Do we need sugar?"

He shook his head, and there was pleasure—maybe anticipation—on his face. "You will like this," he promised again.

Molly carried the mugs, leaving the bag of pastries to her guest. Patient. Whatever. She sensed his need to contribute whatever he could, and gave him the dignity of shuffling to the table with the doughnuts in his long, slim hand. He gave an audible sigh of relief when he sat down, and Molly smiled. "You really do need to take it easy for a few days."

"Take it easy." He smiled. "You say that a lot."

"Because I'm so sure you won't." Molly bent her head to the steam and inhaled it, then lifted the cup and took an experimental sip. Cinnamon and coffee and dark sugar burst on her tongue. "Oh! That's wonderful!" She took another taste—closing her eyes this time. "Mmm." She looked at him with a smile. "Thank you."

She surprised an expression of something she couldn't quite name on his face. Something oddly alert, intense. Then it was gone. She pushed the doughnuts toward him. "Eat, so I can give you medicine."

He picked out a glazed one, lifted his eyebrows at her and dug in. Molly said, "Tell me, *señor,* how it is that you came to be working the fields."

He raised his eyes, and she saw that he was about to make light of it. But suddenly something in his face shifted, and that intense expression came back and he said softly, "*Señora,* you have beautiful eyes."

Startled, Molly looked away, strangely pierced. Then she lifted her head again. "Thank you," she said in a calm voice. "So do you."

He grinned. "But very different, huh?"

"Yes." She picked up her doughnut and urged him to do the same. "Now tell me your story, *señor.*"

"Please," he said. "Call me Alejandro."

She nodded, but didn't say the word. Not yet. It would roll on her tongue, lilt in her mouth, and she wasn't ready to taste it. It would have been much better, she thought, if he'd been named Hector or Porfino.

"My father was a businessman. We, my sisters and I, had everything." He caught her skeptical expression. "Ah, you don't believe me."

She inclined her head. "Maybe. Go on."

"I went to very good schools, in Mexico City, and so did my sisters, off to boarding school, you know?" He eyed his doughnut and took a bite, chewed it slowly, then asked, "That was after they found oil, and everybody thought Mexico would be a rich, rich country."

"Oil?" She associated oil with the Middle East.

"Much oil—and it could have been the thing that turned the country around." He started to sigh, then cut off midbreath and reflexively put a hand to his ribs. "But there was poor management, too many loans. The government crashed." He carefully wiped his fingers on a napkin. "My father went down with it. Lost everything."

"How old were you?"

"Fifteen. It wasn't so bad for me. I never liked it, school. I wanted to be with the land. So, my uncle, he took us in. He was not rich, like my father, but not poor, either. He had a good farm. It was good enough."

Molly discovered that she liked the way he talked. His voice was not deep, but the lilting accent, the precise emphasis he put on certain consonants appealed to her. "But?" she prompted.

He bent his head. "My younger sister, she was—" He shook his head. "She wanted too much. A rich life. A boy came to marry her. A good man, I think, but ordinary, a farmer. She ran away." He looked away, into the distance, into the past. Light shimmered on the dark irises. "To America."

"Land of the free and home of the brave," Molly said, tongue in cheek.

He lifted a shoulder. "Land of money. She thought she would come here and find some man who had plenty of money to marry her and take care of her, and she would have—" a dry lift of his eyebrows as he gestured toward her kitchen "—this."

Molly felt a curious sense of guilt. But that was silly. Wasn't it?

Alejandro continued, "You can guess what happened to her." The beautiful mouth tightened. "She worked for three dollars an hour as a maid for a big hotel in Texas. It was okay, you know? She was happy enough. Sent money back to us sometimes, like she was the *rica*."

Molly smiled. "So where is she now?"

"She married. Not rich, but she had a dishwasher."

A sad smile. "She had Josefina, too. An American citizen. But it turned out her husband was no good. She left him when Josefina was only two. It was hard for her, but she wanted to stay so Josefina could have something better. So she would be an American."

He took a breath and wiped his fingers on a napkin. "Two years ago, my sister was killed in a car accident. Josefina was with the baby-sitter. She called us to say what happened."

Again, sorrow settled like a veil over his features. "My sister had asked, a long time before, if I would go to America and take care of her daughter if something happened." He lifted a shoulder. "So I came. In a van, in the night. And here I am still."

Molly sipped her coffee, letting the story settle. A soft sense of admiration went through her, that a man would honor a promise that caused him so much personal difficulty. "Why not apply for citizenship?"

His smile was bitter and knowing. He did not even bother with a reply, only shook his head.

Molly knew a little of the problems of Mexican nationals gaining citizenship in the United States. Given the political and social impact of such immigrants on the local economy, as well as the ancient Spanish colonial roots of the region, the subject was in the news a lot. "I guess you aren't a Nobel prize–winning scientist, huh?" she said lightly.

He rewarded her with a grin. And this time, it wasn't a small quirk of the lips, but the whole thing. White teeth in a half moon, a wide, flashing grin. It hit her the same way it had last night—right through the solar plexus. "No scientist," he said, and spread his strong brown hands, palm up. "Only a horseman and a farmer. Plenty here already."

"I'm sorry," Molly said impulsively.

He shrugged. "I tried, you know, to find someone to marry me. For money. And there was an old woman, in Colorado, who was going to do the paperwork for me another time, so I could help her with her yard." He shook his head.

Molly noticed suddenly that he was still sweating, and his left arm stayed protectively wrapped around his ribs. "Let me get you some more medicine," she said. "And then you should go back to bed."

"What I would like, *señora,* very much, is to bathe." He inclined his head, modestly, and met her gaze. "I do not think I can do it alone."

"I'll help you," she said matter-of-factly. "I'm only sorry I didn't think of it myself." She stood and held out a hand. "It will make you feel better."

He looked at his hands.

Molly chuckled. "I won't look," she said. "Much."

A smile edged his mouth, abashed and accepting. Molly helped him to his feet.

His saint put her strong shoulder under his arm again, and helped him down the hall. It was easier with her, easier on his pains, anyway. Not so easy in some other ways. From his vantage point above her, the crown of her blond and brown and gilt hair was visible, but so was the top swell of her breasts. He tried not to look, but each time he moved his eyes, it seemed there was that slope of smooth white flesh again. Nothing on earth would have aroused him exactly in his current state, but if he could have been, that slope of smooth pale skin would have more than done it.

Up close, she smelled of wind and sage and soap. Faint hints of cinnamon came from her breath. Her braid slithered along his arm, silky and heavy at once, and he wondered how her hair looked when it was not braided.

She led him to a bathroom that he had not seen. This was big, nearly as big as his bedroom at the farm, and it was not like any room he'd seen before. Warm pine panels covered the walls, varnished carefully to seal the moisture out. A huge old tub on claw feet dominated one corner. Plants hung around skylights and a ring of windows along the top of the wall. "Very nice," he said.

"My husband's pride and joy." She settled him on the closed lid of the toilet. "He was a carpenter."

He glanced down, and saw the wedding ring still lived on her left hand. Choosing not to ask his questions, he said only, "A good one."

She straightened, looking around with pleasure as she efficiently tied her braid in a knot. The position put her breasts in silhouette, and he saw they were shaped like commas, heavier at the bottom curve.

"Yes, he was," she said, and met his eyes, answering the question he had not asked. "I'm a widow. He died four years ago."

"I am sorry."

A sad smile. "Me, too." Briskly, she bent over and dropped a plug in the drain and turned on the water. "Nice and hot?"

Alejandro nodded.

"What we're going to do here is—" she opened a linen closet and took out a pile of towels she set on the sink "—you can undress to your skivvies, and I'll help you with whatever you can't manage, then leave you to the rest."

"Skivvies?"

"Underwear. Then I'll bring you fresh clothes and you can manage the covering-up part, and I'll help you get dressed." She smiled. "Okay?"

Her attitude was so sensible it made his modesty seem foolish. He lifted his shoulder, caught his breath against the pain that spread in a band over his chest and said in a strangled voice, "Okay."

Her laughter was soft. "Come on, big boy, hand over the shirt."

It was not nearly as humiliating as he'd feared. Her no-nonsense hands braced him as he undressed to his "skivvies" and her strong, small body provided the support he needed to get into the tub. He could not suppress a groan of pleasure as he sank into the water.

"Too hot?"

"No, no. Perfect."

"Maybe the heat will ease some of your stiffness. Let me get your hair washed and I'll leave you to soak a little while."

"Oh, you do not need—"

"Alejandro."

It was the first time she had said his name, and in her softly husky voice, it was beautiful. He raised his eyes. She looked down at him, a patient expression on her mouth. "You can't wash your hair. You can't lift your arms."

"No," he admitted.

"Do me a favor." She knelt beside the tub, putting her face on the same level as his own. "I'm a nurse. I do these things all the time. Stop being humiliated every time you run into something you can't do, okay?"

A wave of gratitude overtook him. Gripping his knees with his hands, he met her gaze. "When this is done, you must promise you will let me repay you for your great kindness, Saint Molly. Okay?''

"Okay." She grinned. "Now let me wash your hair."

She dippered water into a cup and poured it over his head. "Close your eyes."

He did. And finally, he took her advice, too. He gave himself up to letting her take care of him. He let the tension and grief and worry drain from his neck as her fingers worked over his scalp. As if the water washed away his negative emotions along with the grime of two days from his skin, he felt peace invade him. Her fingers were strong, working in the shampoo, then conditioner that smelled of musk. She rinsed it out, pushing his long hair back from his face, and he heard a soft sound come from her. He opened his eyes.

She ducked her head, hiding her expression, and reached for the soap. "I'm going to do your back, then leave you to the rest."

Was that breathlessness for him? He turned to look at her, suddenly feeling the intimacy of the moment, of himself wet and nearly naked, with a woman he had never seen forty-eight hours ago. Steam came off his limbs and the water, making her skin damp and flushed. The T-shirt clung to her breasts and waist, outlining a very female figure that Alejandro suddenly wanted to touch. He was suddenly aware of his body, not the pain in it, but the shape of his shoulders and chest, of his legs sticking out of the water, of his back. He wondered if she found him pleasing, and looked for that knowledge on her face.

But she did not allow it. She ducked behind him, rubbing his back in circles with the soapy cloth, then efficiently rinsing it off. Then, abruptly, she stood.

"Finish up," she said, pushing a tendril of hair off her face with a wet hand. "I'll be back in a few minutes."

Perplexed, he nodded, and stared after her as she bolted.

Then he leaned back in the water, gently so as not to jar the faraway state of his assorted aches, and let the heat seep into him, all the way to his bones.

In the hallway, Molly halted and fell against the wall. Air cooled her sweaty, humid skin, but her heart still raced and her hands were definitely trembling. She took a breath, blew it out slowly, feeling a tingle in her ears, all the way around the edge, making them hot. She lifted her hands to them, and found her hands were still wet. She hadn't even bothered to dry them.

In her years as a nurse, she had bathed hundreds— probably thousands—of patients. Old and young, male and female. There was a trick to keeping the mind distant, apart, not only for the nurse, but to preserve the privacy and dignity of the patient.

And she'd been in control with Alejandro until he raised his head, and all at once she'd seen the entirety of his revealed, wet skin, with rivulets of water pooling in the hollow of his collarbone, coursing along the geography of his arm muscles. She'd seen his perfectly shaped ear and the blade of his nose and the high forehead and his wet hair, slicked away from his face by her own hands. In one turn of a second she was not a nurse bathing a patient, but a woman bewitched by an utterly stunning man.

She moved her hands from her ears to her face. Her breasts felt thick and heavy, and her hips were soft. All too clearly, she could see herself returning to that room and putting her mouth to the round place where his arm and shoulder met. She could see her hand spreading open on that chest, scattered with dark hair.

Stop. For the second time in one day, she told herself to just quit it. Get ahold of herself.

This time, she tried a more realistic approach. Taking her hands away from her face, she marched to her bedroom and the bureau, yanking open a drawer with more force than necessary, and delivered a lecture to herself as she tossed through the clothes.

One: she was overstimulated. This interlude had been more exciting than anything that had happened to her in years. A mysterious stranger with a heart-breaking quest had landed in her lap and required care. Needed her.

Two: he was absolutely, drop-dead gorgeous. Any woman who didn't respond to that much virile heat in one package was comatose or dead. She was neither; in fact, she was a widow, a healthy woman in her prime.

Three: she had not had sex in four years. Four years. It was a long time. A really long time. A really, *really* long time.

She caught her wry, amused expression in the mirror over the dresser and it made her grin. The reflection smiled back. Molly noticed that her hair was springing out of its braid and the front of her shirt was wet—had he noticed? He certainly had not seemed to. He was, in fact, singularly unmoved by his nurse. Often men in his situation would think they were attracted to a woman, simply because she'd saved his life. Alejandro appeared to have no such illusions.

She chuckled and stripped off the wet T-shirt, thinking it was probably better if he wasn't attracted to her. Less dangerous all the way around.

From the drawer she took a fresh blouse. Again she caught sight of herself in the mirror, and stopped. *Ordinary* was a good word. Slim shoulders, a good stomach that showed no signs yet of pooching out. Good thing, she thought, touching the expanse of belly over her jeans. Wouldn't take much pooch to overshadow her breasts. She touched them, too, and remembered, for one blinding second, what it had felt like to have her husband's hands on her. How much he'd liked coming up behind her at moments like this. She would lean back, into his broad, strong chest, and lift her hands to his neck, letting him admire the look of his hands on her breasts in the mirror.

The memory was vivid—and in seconds, sharply painful. She dropped her hands, half ashamed, half yearning. With a sigh, she pulled on her shirt. Tim was gone. Gone. Someday maybe she'd get that through her head.

Taking a fresh shirt and sweats, she returned to the bathroom and knocked. "Are you finished?"

No answer.

"Alejandro?" Still nothing. Worried, she knocked once more for the sake of warning and opened the door.

Inside, she stopped and smiled. He had fallen asleep. His hands draped over the edges of the tub and his head was cradled on the little pillow she'd glued to the back, and his knees were akimbo. A glaze of moisture covered the beautiful face, and she felt a prick of something besides desire. He pushed so hard, this man, pushed out of pride and honor. The least she could do was serve that honor as well as she could. Get him well and send him on his way.

She bent over him. Reached out to touch his face. "Come on, *viejo*," she said gently. "Let's get you back to bed."

Chapter 5

Josh stopped by the pharmacy at Judson's to pick up some medicine for the kids. "Hey, George," he said to the thin, graying man behind the counter. "Lynette told me you had some cough syrup for my rug-rats. Is it ready?"

"Sure is." He looked over his reading glasses to measure something. "Damn near everybody's down with this crud, you notice?"

"It's been pretty hairy, all right." Josh leaned on the counter and glanced toward the toy section, eyeing a baby doll with red skirts. Both kids had been miserable for days—maybe he could pick up a toy for each of them. Raise their spirits.

He counted the money from his front pocket. A five, three ones and a twenty. Maybe. "How much is that medicine gonna run?" he asked.

"Well, let's see. Your co-payment is ten, isn't it?"

He punched something into the computer. "Yep. Just ten."

Josh paid for the cough syrup. "I guess I should count my blessings. At least my job has benefits."

"That's right." George opened the register. "How's your sister doing, by the way? Saw her last night, and she had to refill her prescription for antibiotics. Nasty sore throat."

"Last night?" Josh frowned. Last night, she'd bought him a steak and chattered his ear off. If she'd been sick, she sure hadn't looked it. "I don't know. I'll have to give her a call."

The man gave Josh his change, a crisp ten-dollar bill, and he tucked it in his pocket, frowning as he wandered over to check the price on the doll. Molly sick? He didn't think so. Why had she lied?

He picked up the doll and looked for the price. Thirty-two dollars. He put it back, and wandered down another aisle of pink stuff. In the end, he picked out a doctor kit for Rochelle and a sticker book for Danny— both together didn't burn the whole ten-dollar bill he used to pay, and it made him feel better.

Until, on his way out, he saw a Mexican national— you could always tell, they were so much smaller, so much darker than the Hispanic population here—buying that thirty-two-dollar doll.

He tried. On the way to the parking lot, he combated the rising burn in his gut by telling himself the guy probably just got paid and was sending a special treat back home. Maybe it was his daughter's birthday.

But it didn't help. The fact remained: the other guy's kid got the doll. Rochelle got a lousy doctor kit. It wasn't fair.

As he started the truck, he wondered again what was

going on with his sister. She was acting weird. Maybe he'd stop by the hospital on the way home and see what he could find out.

Late in the day, Alejandro stirred again. And this time, he did not feel as if he were swimming through a murky density of pain and confusion. He was aware immediately of the cautionary band of pain around his chest, but it was subdued.

His head was clear. He blinked, testing it, and realized that the latest nap had restored something he'd barely noticed was missing—his sense of himself and his place in the world. He felt as if he'd really slept, instead of simply sliding into unconsciousness.

Carefully, he stood up and found new strength in his limbs, found he could limp gently on his gun-shot leg without too much agony, and his ribs did not jolt unless he moved too quickly.

Progress.

The long glass door in the kitchen stood open, the drapes pulled aside to reveal the small plots of land carefully planted with flowers and what he thought might be herbs. Twilight leaked into the edges of the sky.

And sitting on the steps of the wide porch was his Saint Molly. He leaned against the wall for a moment, startled by his reaction to the simple act she indulged.

She was brushing her hair.

It was beautiful. Very long, draping over her shoulders and falling down her back. She brushed it idly, slowly, as if it pleased her to feel the bristles on her scalp, then she rolled her head and the hair slid and swished over her arms and back, and he could tell she was enjoying the feel of it on her body.

A pulse beat softly just below his ribs, and he found himself remembering the shape of her breasts when she'd tied up her hair this morning. A sudden acute and vivid imagining appeared in his head, a detailed vision of that gilt and sunlight and earthen hair draped over her naked breasts.

He discovered he was not beyond arousal any longer. He was likely beyond *acting* on it, but his body seemed to have no trouble expressing its approval. Taking a breath, he looked away and counted silently, until the edge of it eased.

Then he limped through the kitchen to the door. *"Buenas tardes,"* he said quietly. "Is it safe for me to join you outside, *señora?"*

She turned, and her hair shifted, some of it spilling down her front, bringing back that erotic vision. *"Sí,"* she replied, smiling gently. *"Por favor."*

He eyed the steps dubiously, and she leaped up, extended her hand. Alejandro took it. In his big, dark one, hers was slim and held the illusion of fragility. Illusion only, for he'd experienced that strength, experienced it now as she braced him, helped him ease down one step so he could sit with her.

She settled one step below him. He looked out at the gloaming, feeling something quiet in him. And Molly did not speak, either, seemingly content with the soft chatter of birds in a tree and the distant whisper of an awakening cricket.

Suddenly, the cicadas clicked on, a thousand score of them, roaring to life on the same note, all at the same instant, their music a sonnet in the graying world. Alejandro looked at the trees, knowing the insects would be invisible, but looking anyway, as he always did. They whirred in their rhythmic way for a few minutes, then as suddenly as they'd begun, cut off with the finality of a conductor's baton. He grinned and spread his hands, palm down. "Finished!"

"Don't you always wonder how they know to start and stop like that? So many of them, all at once."

Once he had known, but he couldn't remember now. "I do."

Just beyond his knee, the extravagance of her hair spilled down her back, and he inched his fingers along his thigh, aching to brush his fingertips over it. "You look very young with your hair down."

Self-consciously, she gathered a handful of it. "Think so? I keep thinking lately it's time to cut it. My mother always said a woman should cut her hair when she was thirty."

"Ah, no. You should not cut such hair." He reached out, paused. "May I touch it?"

"Oh. Sure." She leaned a little closer and he took a thick hank into his grip, then let it spill through his fingers, admiring the glitter of it against his dark fingers. It was almost weightless, and very soft, and he liked it very much.

When it nearly fell away, he caught it again, with the other hand, and spread a handful over his open palm. "It makes me think of honeycomb, all these different colors in it." He raised his eyes. "I like it."

A guarded expression warned him away. "Thank you," she said, almost stiffly.

Alejandro, vaguely disappointed, let her hair fall, and shifted his gaze to the fields stretching beyond the gardens. Empty fields, overgrown with gray-green sage and walking stick cactus with hard knots of dark red fruit at the tips. "Is this your land?"

"Some of it." She pointed. "From the bluff over

there, to the cottonwood. Then some more in front of the house.''

He narrowed his eyes, nodding. ''How much land?''

''Close to a hundred acres.''

So much! If he owned land, he would not leave it fallow this way. ''It is good land here,'' he said. ''You do not plant it?''

''My husband had made plans to,'' she said slowly. ''I wouldn't have the faintest idea where to start.''

''Ah.'' He nodded. Still, ''You should do something with it.''

She looked over her shoulder. ''Like what?''

Alejandro inclined his head. ''A henhouse, over there, for eggs. And a rooster to make more chickens—'' he grinned ''—and to wake up the morning. Some goats, for their milk, and some sheep, for the wool.'' He pursed his lips. ''And then the fields...chiles and beans and maybe some pimentos, no? Enough for you, and some to take to market.''

She had a faint smile on her face. ''Anything else?''

He raised an eyebrow, aware she was teasing him. ''Yes. Bees.'' He gestured to the bluff. ''They would feed on the peach trees, and the honey would be very good.''

''I'm afraid of bees.''

''You would learn,'' he replied confidently. ''And with those things, you would not have to work. You would have everything here.''

This time she chuckled. ''But I like working. I'm a much better nurse than I am a farmer.''

The sound of a car engine made them both turn toward the road. Dust kicked up behind a truck, still quite distant but unmistakably headed their way.

''Damn.'' Molly leaped to her feet. ''That's my

brother. We have to get you inside. Fast.'' Worry made her eyes dark gray. ''He's a deputy sheriff, and he won't be happy when he finds out I've done this.''

He started to rise at the same instant she did, and their foreheads cracked together painfully. Molly made a soft noise, and reeled backward, put off balance. Alejandro, blinking against the sharp rap himself, reached out to keep her from falling. He snared her upper arm and yanked, and she tilted forward, a hand coming down on his shoulder. ''Sorry,'' she said. ''Are you okay?''

She was close. But for once, she was not beneath him or beside him. She was not washing him or tending him or feeding him. She faced him, her mouth only inches from his own, her breasts at a level with his hands, and he wanted very much to kiss her, to lift his hands to that inviting weight and gauge her fit to his palms. The wish swelled through him, quick and hot.

As if his thoughts showed on his face, she... softened. It was the only word. The slope of her shoulders eased, and her hand opened wider on his shoulder, as if she'd like to slide her fingers beneath his collar. Her eyelids flickered, sweeping down to hide the direction of her gaze, which he felt on his mouth.

He saw her catch her breath, and for a long second, Alejandro thought she would sway closer and press her mouth to his. He found himself ready, lifting his head, ready to touch her if she gave leave.

Instead, her hand clenched and she gripped him, looking over her shoulder. ''Now, Alejandro. I'm not kidding. He'll arrest you.''

Molly heard her brother's truck on the gravel outside just as she closed her back bedroom door. Alejandro put his fingers to his lips to show her he understood, and she rushed down the hallway, smoothing her hair, trying to breathe normally.

Going out on the front porch, she crossed her arms. "Hey there," she said jauntily as Josh climbed out. Still dressed in his uniform, he looked weary and rumpled and impossibly young. "What brings you out here?"

"Just checking on you. They said you called in sick this morning. You sick?"

Molly had almost forgotten. "I'm feeling better tonight."

He climbed up to the porch, hat in his hands. "How about pouring me a glass of tea, then?"

As she led him into the house, for an odd, scared moment, she thought there was something in his manner that was a little off kilter. His mouth was tight as he looked around—carefully, she thought—at the living room. But she looked again and only saw her brother. Paranoia.

She did not particularly want to lead him into the kitchen—if Alejandro so much as sneezed, Josh would hear it. She directed him to a living-room chair, but he gave her a weird look and followed her into the kitchen, tossing his hat down on the table. "Damn, I'm tired." He flung his lean body into a chair. "You hear anything more about that little girl you were asking about?"

Molly shook her head. "You, neither, huh?"

"Sorry." He accepted the glass of tea she offered him and took a long swallow. "Lynette wants to know if you can have dinner with us Saturday night." He lifted an eyebrow. "If you're feeling all right by then."

He knew something. What? She made a show of

looking at her work schedule on the wall. "I'd love to, especially if she makes her green chile. I could live on her chile."

"She knows. She bought a bushel from Wiley this morning. Said she thought she saw your car up there, but she didn't see you anywhere."

Uh-oh. Molly decided to stick with the truth as much as possible. "I was checking to see if he might have seen that little girl."

"For somebody who had to miss work and get some heavy-duty antibiotics, you sure were busy today."

The pharmacist. Of course. She could just imagine how it had gone, too. "Is there a point to all this, Josh? I feel like a suspect or something."

"No point." He crossed his ankle on his knee. "You just seemed a little weird last night, kind of nervous or something. Then I hear you've got some bad sore throat, and you don't go to work, and then you're up at Wiley's asking questions. If it's innocent, there's nothing to worry about, is there? If you've got a guilty conscience, it's my business to find out what you're hiding."

She struggled to keep her features even, but the words made her cold, and she realized she'd underestimated her brother's deep, wide knowledge of her.

And then, with a cat's superior timing, Leonardo came trotting down the hall with a sock in his mouth. A very large white tube sock with a blue stripe around the top. It trailed between his legs, making it hard for him to walk, and he dropped it once, then picked it up again and headed for the dining room.

Frozen, Molly couldn't decide whether to ignore her cat or make a production of him. She aimed for something in between. Rolling her eyes, she grimaced.

"Who would I be hiding? Some desperado? Some drug dealer?"

"I don't know. Interesting, though, that you thought immediately of a person. I didn't say who, I said what."

Damn. She was really not cut out for lying. She forced herself not to look at Leo, who now tossed the incriminating sock up in the air. Unable to think of a single thing to answer her brother with, she shrugged.

Just then, he let go of the deputy sheriff mask and his whole body eased with the reappearance of Josh-the-brother. "Look, Moll, I know you. You've always got some cause, and don't think I haven't paid attention to your feelings on this whole illegal-immigrant issue. I know we're on opposite sides of the line, and I just keep quiet about it for that reason. But if you've done something you want to tell me about, I'm here as your brother." He picked up his hat. "This time."

"Okay, Joe Friday. I'll be sure and let you know if I see any suspicious characters lurking in my alleys."

"Moll—"

She raised a hand. "I'm just kidding. When did you get so damned serious, anyway? I remember the wild child."

"I grew up fast when Mom and Dad were killed. Didn't seem right to give you the trouble I gave them."

"Honey, it was real sad, but that was more than a decade ago." She touched his bony shoulder. "You can loosen up now. Have some fun, huh?"

He nodded noncommittally, and Molly dropped her hand. "Thanks for your concern," she said, walking him to the door. "I'll see you on Saturday night."

On the porch, he put his hat back on and paused. "Be careful, Molly."

Molly laughed, hoping it sounded free instead of nervous. "I will."

He gave the house and surrounding lands one last, sweeping search with his eyes, then lifted a hand in farewell. She forced herself to stand there, ostensibly admiring the view of ragged mountains against a nearly dark sky, until he was out of sight.

Then she let go of a shaky breath and went inside, first going to the corner to retrieve the white tube sock from Leo's stash. He blinked when she wrested the sock from him, and settled on top of the others as if to protect them. "You're one strange cat, Leo."

She knocked on the back bedroom door. Alejandro called out, and she opened the door to find him sitting on the bed, his boots on beneath the sweats, looking glumly at the combination. "Missing something?" she said, holding the stolen socks.

"Oh, yes. Thank you."

"Leonardo—that's my cat—steals socks. He gave me a heart attack just now, dragging this one out in front of my brother."

"*Señora,* I am sorry to have caused you so much trouble." With a grunt, he managed to get his right leg into position to take off the boot, and struggled with it.

Molly knelt and grabbed the heel. "Pull." The boot came off, revealing his naked foot. She was annoyed with herself for liking the strong, long bones across the high arch. "I guess you heard all that, huh?"

He nodded, and busied himself with pulling on the sock. "Your husband—did he have jeans?" One side of his mouth lifted in distaste. "This does not look right."

"He did." Molly perched in the mama chair, hiding

a smile that he could be vain enough to worry about
his outfit when he was gun-shot, rib-broke and wanted
by the law. "I'm not turning you out, though."

He raised large black eyes to her face and echoed,
"Turning me out?"

"You don't have to leave."

He took a breath. "I do. I heard what he said,
Molly." His tongue caressed the word, making it
longer, lingering: Mol-leee. "He will be very angry
when he learns you have hidden me here."

"If," she corrected calmly. "And yes, he'll be furious, but he'll be furious no matter if you stay a day
or three. The damage is done."

"They might arrest you." His mouth was serious.
"Deport me."

She nodded. Then, without consciously deciding to
do it, she leaned over her knees and in a gesture that
felt wholly natural, took his loose hands into her own.
"Señor Sosa, please listen." She met his eyes earnestly. "My brother worries too much about me."

"If you were my sister, I, too, would worry. It is
only luck that I am not a drug dealer, as you say."

"Maybe." She lifted a shoulder. "But the fact re-
mains—you aren't. And you feel better tonight, but if
you leave now, you'll be sick and cold and weak by
morning. You won't be any use to Josefina like that."

He looked at the clasp of her hands, and suddenly
turned his over, enfolding her fingers in his. "You listen, now, *señora,*" he said, and leaned closer still, so
their faces were only a foot apart. A soft hitch of desire
touched her heart as she looked at his mouth, into his
eyes, and she wanted, very much, to simply close that
gap and press her mouth to his.

And as if the same thought crossed his mind, his

gaze flickered to her mouth, then away. His jaw tightened. "I am very grateful to you. You have saved my life. And you have taken good care of me. I do not wish to bring trouble on you. Maybe Wiley would take me in, eh? It's not so far, I could walk there."

A pang stabbed through her. Wiley probably would take him in, but that would mean this stolen time was over. Just another day. Maybe two, that was all she asked. A little space of time that was different from all the other days in her life. "Maybe," she said quietly.

It was her turn to look at the tangle of their hands. She turned his over to look at the palms, seeing calluses along the tips of his long fingers. She touched the thickened skin lightly. "Do you play guitar?"

"Yes." For a moment, he allowed her touch, then abruptly drew away. "Molly, will you bring me the jeans from your husband?"

"Sure." She stood up, pasting a bright, phony smile on her face as she stood up. "I'll be right back."

Before she turned away, however, he stood and caught her hand. It was the first time she realized how very tall and lean and powerful his body was. She raised her face to meet his liquid gaze, waiting, unable to hide the disappointment she felt, no matter how irrational it was.

He peered at her, perplexed. "You do not wish for me to leave."

She hesitated, then shook her head, but that seemed to require that she offer a reason. It would save her trouble in the long run. Why didn't she want him to go?

A rush of answers whirled in her mind, most of them half-formed—because he was beautiful and she wanted to be near him. Because he had touched something in her that had been dead a long time, and made it alive again. Because—

"I'll worry," she said simply. "If you get a little more rest, show a little more caution, I won't have to think of you out there in the cold, hurting."

A hint of a smile touched his mouth. "You would spare so much thought on a wanderer? A—how did you say it?—desperado." His tongue put the right accents on the word, and it sounded much more dangerous. A picture rose in her mind of a desert and a man on a horse and a perilous full moon hanging in the endless sky.

"I would spare that much thought for you," she said.

The words caused a subtle shift in the air. He did not move, but she suddenly felt him more, felt the warmth of him along her body, sensed the shape of his lean hips and wide shoulders. Felt, too, her breath soften in her chest, as if in readiness.

He raised his right hand and pressed the backs of his fingers to her cheek, lightly. "Then I will stay."

Josefina was afraid. She was cold. The wind was picking up and she was frightened of the shadows it sent skittering over the land. Even her little dog seemed afraid, because he whined and huddled closer to her, both of them clasped in her stolen blanket.

At dark, they had gone down to the dairy bar again and she spent almost all of her five-dollar bill on hot dogs and hot chocolate and candy. They each had a hot dog and she found an old milk carton in the trash, which she filled with water for the dog. Josefina put the candy in her pocket for later and they walked back toward the orchard, shivering a little in the wind. It made her cough.

That scared her. All day, she had been coughing more. And it hurt more. And she didn't feel so good. Once, during the summer, she had been very sick with this cough for many days. She couldn't remember very much of what happened then—it was all jumbled in her head with strange images of fire and rockets. Tío told her it was the Fourth of July when she was sick.

She was very afraid it was going to be like that again. There was that softness in her brain again, and the world looked funny, sparkly. She was even more afraid when she saw that it was no longer the thin fluid her cough ordinarily brought up, but there was blood, too.

And tonight, it was cold. She felt the wind cutting through her shirt like a knife, slicing up her skin like a tomato. She was afraid to sleep in the cold. How could she get a blanket?

The idea was bad. She knew it even when she thought it up. But on the way to the dairy bar was a washing place. People took in their clothes and put in the money, then went next door to shop, or across the street to the bar.

Josefina wandered in and acted as if she was supposed to be there. Her little dog followed her in, his head down, as if he was afraid somebody would kick him. Nobody said anything. There was only an old lady with her black hair in a bun, putting aprons in a dryer.

It took a long time, but Josefina had plenty. She looked at old, messed-up magazines and ate a little of her candy. She used the bathroom, happy to have a real toilet, and while she was in there, she washed her face and hands. The world seemed dizzier and dizzier as the evening wore on, but at least it was warm in here.

At last she had her chance. A man with a belly like a barrel put a bunch of things in washers. Everything. Coats and socks. Blankets. He washed them, then came back after a while, smelling like the workers on Saturday nights, and put everything in the dryers. Josefina sat on her hands, humming a little when she didn't cough, though that was getting harder and harder. She had to get a tissue from the bathroom to cover her mouth with.

"Where's your mama, girl?" the man asked.

Josefina gave him her most guileless stare. "*No hablo inglés.*"

He looked worried for a minute, acted as if he was going to say something else, but Josefina just glared at him, and he shrugged and left.

She had to wait another half hour, but then the blanket was dry, and the man had not come back. She looked outside, both ways, to be sure, then opened the dryer, grabbed the striped blanket, hot from the air inside, and ran out, her little dog following behind.

Molly and Alejandro ate a simple meal, during which Alejandro seemed to grow more and more restless, his attention on his missing niece. She had heard the weather report, and worried right along with him, but everything that could be done had been, and until morning, she didn't know what else to do.

"You know," she said finally. "If she doesn't surface by say, noon tomorrow, I'll go to the sheriff."

He frowned. "But your brother—"

"He's a deputy." She pressed her mouth together. "If I take it to the sheriff himself, I'm going to have to tell him the truth—that you're worried. Otherwise, they're just going to pat me on the head and send me on my way.''

His jaw tightened. ''I am very worried about her. Better she is in a home than out there.'' Sorrow filled his eyes. ''She will be very sad.''

Molly considered. ''If they deport you, how long will it take you to get back?''

''A few days. A week, maybe.''

''Okay—this is what we'll do, then. If Josefina is still missing in the morning, I'll go to the sheriff and he can start a search. If you end up getting deported, I'll ask to keep her here.''

He lowered his eyes, laced his fingers together. ''Thank you.''

''It won't be for long.''

When he lifted his face, there was weariness in it, lying in the hollows of his cheeks. ''I hate to live this way. Sometimes, I think it would be better for Josefina to take her home to Mexico, to my uncle, where we would not have to hide.'' He spread his hands and looked at them, as if they contained the future—or maybe the past. ''It was a good life. I miss it very much.''

She thought of his description of what she should do with her land, and smiled. ''Did you have goats for their milk? And sheep for their wool?''

He grinned. ''*Sí*. And chickens for eggs.''

''And a rooster for morning.''

''It's a good alarm clock, no? Not like those bells.''

''I wouldn't know.''

''Try it one day. You will see.''

She hesitated, but only for a moment. ''Why don't you take her back to your home, then?''

He lifted his shoulders. "My sister wanted her to be here. To be an American. She died for that, you know?"

"Yeah." Molly inclined her head, wondering how to delicately phrase her question. "But wouldn't it be better for Josefina in Mexico? She could go to school. Be in one place."

He made a soft snorting sound and leaned, wincing only a little, over the table. "When I first came here, those first few weeks, I was shocked every day. Women do anything here." He paused. "Not in Mexico." His eyes focused on something distant. "And Josefina—she's very smart. She already reads big books, and her teacher last summer, in the camp, was very mad that I could not take her to a normal school. She said Josefina was—" he lifted his hand, as if trying to pull the word from the air "—*dotada,* I can't think of it in English." He touched his temple. "Very smart in mathematics."

"*Dotada,*" Molly echoed, liking the sound of the word. "I don't know what it means, but I get the idea."

He smiled. "Say like this," and he repeated it.

Molly tried again and was rewarded with a nod of approval. "*Bueno.*"

She tried not to beam too much at his approval, and reminded herself to look up the word. Gifted, maybe? It brought her thoughts back to the little girl, alone and cold out there somewhere. As if she might spot her, she looked over her shoulder to the dark pane of glass facing the gardens. "Is it so impossible for you to get a visa, Alejandro? There's nothing?" She hesitated. "Is there anyone I could write, on your behalf?"

"God made you to nurse the world, I think." He put his hand over hers. "From the bottom of my heart, I

thank you, Saint Molly. But there is no one to write.''
He smiled now, sadly. "I have already tried.''

She nodded, sighed and gently pulled away, picking
up dishes to carry to the sink. "You know, this whole
subject is in the news all the time. Laws about it.'' She
lifted a hand, staring out at the vast emptiness that was
the northern New Mexico vista.

His mouth turned down and he lifted his coffee cup.
"I do not blame anyone here. People wish to protect
what they have, no? And if the politicos in Mexico
would do what they should, we would not need to run
here.''

"Yeah. It's a complicated issue.''

"No,'' he said quietly. "It is simple, really. As long
as America is here, so much richer, there will be Mex-
icans who come.''

Molly smiled. "That does make it sound simple.''
To shift the direction of the conversation away from
politics, she said, "I've wanted to travel in Mexico.
What's it like?''

"In the north, much of it is like this.'' He spread his
hands toward the door. "But then it gets better. Where
I lived, the land is rich. We grow many things, and sell
them to the exporters—you know, who make frozen
vegetables?''

"And what made it a good life?''

He inclined his head, making that hair fall a little to
one side. Light caught on the glossiness, and Molly
knew she was only talking to keep him there. But when
he lifted his eyes, frankly, to hers, she decided he
talked in order to stay. "It's a simple world. The days
are the same. It's good, knowing you will wake up in
your bed and the fields will be waiting, and then at
night, we will sit in the back with the dogs, and maybe

some children, and somebody plays guitar.'' He smiled. ''Boring, no?''

''Not at all.'' In fact, she thought his description said a lot about his character. It reinforced her feeling that he was a man of the land, truly born of it, with the rhythms carved in his soul. ''It sounds peaceful.''

''Peaceful. Yes, that's a good word.'' Absently, he touched his ribs.

''Are you in pain?''

''No. Not so much.'' He laughed a little, as if in surprise. ''I was thinking this is a peaceful place, too.''

Molly laughed. ''No, this is really boring. I had to get Leo, the cat, to have some entertainment.'' Apologetically, she lifted a shoulder. ''I don't always like living so far out. I lived in town all my life.''

''So you want the cars in the streets, those lights shining in your window?''

''Not exactly—but I like kids walking by after school. And talking with my neighbors. Having somebody over the back fence.''

The large dark eyes fixed on her face, strangely sober. ''You are lonely. That is why you wanted me to stay.''

Molly ducked her head instantly, but it wasn't quick enough to hide her humiliation. It burned along her ears, and she was grateful for the hair that would cover it.

He touched her hand on the table and said gently, ''I know about lonely, too.''

She couldn't quite bear to look at his face, but his fingertips rested lightly on her fingernails, the lightest possible touch, and she could look there. ''Loneliness,'' she said absently, and raised her head. ''It's lonely and loneliness. One is an adjective, the other a noun.''

"Ah." He nodded, but did not take his hand away. "Same in Spanish. *Solitario* and *soledad*." He tapped her forefinger with his own. "And one more, too. If a place is lonely, it is *aislado*."

"*Aislado*." The word made her think of a desert beneath a full moon, a lone rider crossing in danger. "I like that."

"You are lonely," he said. "I know about loneliness. And this—" he gestured to the door "—is, for you, *aislado*. Can you say that word in English?"

She thought. Shook her head. "No. I don't think there is a word." She lifted a shoulder. "Haunted, maybe."

"Is your land haunted, Molly?"

She thought of the nights when she lay alone in her bed and heard coyotes howling in the distance—and sometimes not so distant. She thought of the emptiness of the fields when they were blanketed in snow, and not a single footstep showed on it for days and days. "No," she said. "*Aislado* is better."

His smile shifted every line, every angle in his face into a new light, putting mischief in his faintly tilted eyes. Molly wondered why it felt so amazingly good to have that zillion-watt grin turned on her.

And at the answer, she was appalled. Loneliness. She had been terribly, terribly lonely out here, and he broke the sameness. He made her smile, and gave her someone to take care of and someone to talk to.

Stiffly, she stood. "You should go back to bed."

Perplexed, he inclined his head. "I offended you."

"No," she said. "I embarrassed myself, that's all, and I'd like a little time to recover my dignity."

He frowned a little, but leaning on the table, pulled himself to a standing position. Molly moved close automatically to offer her shoulder, and he looped his long arm around her, using the wall for additional support.

And though they'd done this several times, Molly found herself a little lost in the sensations tonight. She was aware of his lean hip close to her side, of his wrist against her shoulder, and more than anything, the scent of him, his skin and hair and the warm places.

"Do you want to go to your room, or would you like to watch television or something, maybe?"

"I would like television." His voice didn't show nearly as much strain as it had earlier, and she was taking far less of his weight than she had this morning. He must be prodigiously healthy.

Then she realized he'd walked under his own power to the back door earlier, and she raised her head. "You didn't really need my help this time, did you?"

A wicked glint sparked in the laughing eyes. "*Sí, señora.* I feel so weak."

They'd reached the living room, and she slid away. "You must think I'm very silly."

He laughed, and caught her collar before she could quite get away. "No. I think you are kind." The smile faded a little as he took her hair, now braided tightly, into his hand. "And I did not mean to hurt you when I said you were lonely."

Every word, made oddly musical in his accent, fell like rain on her dry soul. "It's all right." She took a breath. "It's probably true. Lucky for you, huh?"

He let her braid fall. "Yes. Lucky me."

Chapter 6

Molly illustrated the use of the remote control, and aware of an odd, pleased sense of happiness, went back to the kitchen, mouthing *dotada* under her breath, putting her tongue on her teeth in imitation of him, then tried the other words. Especially *aislado*. Great word.

Running the sink full of hot sudsy water, she mused for the millionth time on the fact that, even with all the opportunities around her, she still did not speak very much Spanish. There were four all-Spanish radio stations and two television stations in the area. At least half the people in the valley spoke Spanish—albeit a colonial version that had some inconsistencies—at home and within the community, to each other. Everyone was expected to know the most basic things.

It seemed, with so much opportunity, almost absurd that they weren't all bilingual.

The phone rang as she was drying her hands. Expecting Lynette, Molly answered cheerfully.

"Oh, good," said the voice on the other end of the line. "You sound a lot better."

It was Cathy, the nursing supervisor at the small hospital where Molly worked. Busted. "I am, thanks. It wasn't that bad to start with. I just didn't think I ought to be breathing all over the patients with a virus."

"Well, guess what, doll? I need you. Two more nurses called off tonight, and we're getting slammed. Two moms in labor, a bar fight and two new cases of pneumonia from this damned flu. If you come in tonight, I can probably cover most of tomorrow."

Molly glanced toward Alejandro, torn. But she really couldn't say no. "Sure," she said. "I'd like to have the morning off to get some sleep, but I can work the rest of my normal shift in the afternoon."

"Thanks, kid. You might be able to get out of here after midnight sometime."

"See you in a little bit, then."

Molly went to the living room. "The hospital called," she said. "I have to go to work tonight. Will you be okay?"

"Sure." He held up the remote control. "Movies. TV." Spread his hands, a faint smile on his face. "Couch and pillow. I'm very okay."

"Okay. There's food, too. Help yourself." She started to walk to her room and turned back. "And don't get any brave ideas of striking out on your own. I'll be very worried about you."

He touched his chest, a promise. "I will stay until the morning, Saint Molly."

It was indeed very busy at the hospital. Molly hit the floor running and didn't stop till nearly eleven when the second baby was delivered. By then, after her long night and day, she was yawning so hard her jaw cracked, and her boss sent her to get a cup of coffee. Stirring sugar into the thin brew, she thought of the luscious mixture Alejandro had made—was that only this afternoon?—and made a mental note to have him leave the recipe.

When he moved on. As he would.

She sat in the break room with the door open, and heard the shouts when a new patient came in the emergency exit. With a sigh, she poured out her unfinished cup, wondering if it was the full moon or something, and jogged out into the hall to see what had happened now.

When she saw who it was, she halted abruptly, and it seemed all the systems in her body stopped for a moment, too. It was Wiley, and in his arms, he carried a small bundle of child wrapped in a blanket—a blanket, Molly saw with a tight clutch of fear, that was stained with blood.

She looked at Wiley urgently, and he gave her a slight, small nod.

Her body switched from dead stop to humming overdrive in a flash, and she rushed forward. "Josefina?" she said, pulling back the blanket to see the child's face. "Oh, God!" Blood smeared over one cheek. "Take her in there quickly." She followed, her stethoscope banging against her breasts. "What happened? Where did you find her?"

The farmer settled the child on the bed with more gentleness than she would have expected. "Damnedest thing. A yappy little dog showed up on my back porch just as I was getting ready to go to bed. I opened it to shoo him away, but he backed off, barking his fool head off."

Molly listened as she stripped the blanket away, revealing a very slim child with long black hair, her angled face pale but unmistakably related to Alejandro. She appeared to be unconscious.

"The dog wouldn't be quiet, so I followed him, thinking about what you said." He lifted one gnarled brown hand. "I found her under a tree, just like this. Blood all over her face."

"Has she spoken?"

"Nah. Not really. Just some moaning."

The girl twisted and started to cough, her body pulling into a fetal position as if in protection. It was a violent, spine-wracking cough, and Molly realized where the blood was coming from. Automatically, she grabbed a face mask and tied it around her mouth and nose, handing another to Wiley. "I'll get the doctor in here, and then you can go, but you say that Josefina went to Health Services?"

"Yeah. Don't know what for."

The girl started to shiver, and she twisted again, crying out a name, "Tío!" in a pitifully weak voice. It started a new coughing fit.

The doctor, a tall woman in scrubs, appeared, and started her examination, barking out questions none of them could answer. The child was dehydrated and feverish, but when the doctor listened to her chest, she exchanged a look with Molly—this was not bronchitis or pneumonia, though the girl's condition might have been complicated by one or both. "Let's get an X ray. Now."

"TB?" Molly said quietly.

"Sure looks like it. Let's run the tests, get her blood gases, and get her into isolation." She peered at Wiley. "Where are her people?"

''No idea,'' he said gruffly, pulling at his mustache. ''Might call the sheriff to see if they got him down at the station. Her uncle was a big tall fella, not too old. Name that was familiar somehow—oh, I know, it was Sosa, like that baseball player.''

''Thank you.'' The doctor glanced at Molly. ''Get the kid settled, then let's get Annie to call the sheriff's office and see what we can find out.''

Wiley hesitated at the door. ''What's gonna happen to her?''

Molly tugged the blanket over the child and made preparations to move her. ''Probably Social Services will decide. I'll let you know.''

''Thanks.''

The little girl bolted straight up all at once, her eyes wild. *''Pequeña!''* she cried. ''My dog!'' She gripped Molly's arm almost painfully. *''Dónde está mi perro?''*

''I'll take care of him, sugar. Don't you worry.'' Wiley said, and Molly was oddly moved by his gentleness. ''Put him in a bed all by himself, with some bones. How's that?''

She looked disbelieving and unbearably sad. Molly stroked her head. ''Do you understand?''

''I speak English,'' she said bleakly.

''You can trust him, sweetie.''

The grip eased. She nodded. Molly soothed her back down, and Wiley tipped his hat and left.

Glancing over her shoulder to make sure she was alone, Molly then bent over the child, and took the tiny, frail hand in her own. ''Josefina,'' she said, ''I need to tell you something important. It's very secret, and I can only say it once, so listen carefully, *comprende?''*

''Yes.'' Luminous eyes, fever bright, showed no fear

now. She even patted Molly's hand, as if to reassure her. "I speak English very *well*."

Molly smiled. "Good. You've been looking for your uncle, right?"

A nod.

"I know where he is." The thin fingers tightened convulsively and didn't ease. "He was hurt, just a little, in the raid, and he is not far away." She paused. "No one must know, or he might go to jail. I need you to pretend you know me, okay?"

"My uncle is okay?"

"Yes. He is very worried about you."

"Can he come to me here?"

"I don't know. I'll try."

Another soft nod. "That's your name?" She pointed to the name tag. "Molly?"

"Yeah."

"Thank you, Señora Molly," she said very gravely.

"You're very welcome." She let go and explained what she had to do now, to take care of her. The child endured the needle pokes with good grace, and Molly wheeled her into a room down the hall, with a window and a view of the Rio Grande by day. If she had tuberculosis, she would probably be here for a while.

She washed the girl's face and propped her up, then started the IV tube for rehydration and whatever course of drugs the doctor chose once the results were back. The child, obviously exhausted, fell into a doze, and Molly tenderly tucked her in tightly.

Only then, winded, did she sink down in the silent room to consider what this would mean. Tuberculosis was on the rise throughout the country, and it had been showing up with alarming frequency among several levels of the population, often in cities where people lived close together, and in migrant camps for the same reason. Many, like in Josefina's probable case, were misdiagnosed until the disease was advanced.

If it was indeed TB, Josefina would be quarantined until the active symptoms could be controlled, and then she would have to take a course of treatments that lasted eighteen months.

Molly reeled with the implications. The child was not going anywhere for quite some time. As an American citizen, she'd be placed with Social Services while Alejandro was deported. How could Molly stave it off?

The answer must have been brewing in the back of her mind, because it appeared, simple and terrifying, without much prompting. It also held the potential for a better than moderate humiliation for Molly, who would look even more like a sex-starved widow. She didn't know if Alejandro would even agree—though she suspected he would, to save his niece.

Before she could lose her nerve, Molly jumped up and went to find her supervisor. "I need some help," she said quietly.

"What's up?" Cathy asked.

"Keep Social Services and the law off the little girl in 202, will you? Just till morning."

Her eyes narrowed. "What's going on, Molly? You've been weird for two days."

Molly raised her eyebrows. "I can't tell you right this minute. But I promise I'll have some answers when I come back. Just keep the dogs off the girl for a few hours. Will you?"

"Yeah."

"I'll be back by say...ten?"

Cathy nodded. "All right."

* * *

Alejandro had trouble falling asleep. Each time he lay down, thoughts of Josefina overtook him. Thoughts of her cold. Thoughts of her frightened. And each time, he'd work himself into a panic, wanting to act, and having no act to perform. Fear for her stole his breath.

He looked through the paperback books on one shelf. His reading in English was progressing, and he took a ghost story from the shelves. He considered going to the kitchen to get a glass of water, but it seemed too far for the assembled aches starting to creep back in all over him, and he settled with a blanket over his shoulders for warmth in the living room. The cat jumped up into his lap, a warm, heavy lump. Glad of the company, Alejandro stroked the silky, longish fur.

The reading proved to be more work than it was worth and with a sigh, he put the book aside. Sleep would make time pass faster. And he needed it for healing purposes—he needed to take leave of his saint before he made some move that wounded her, offended her.

At the thought of Molly, however, the tightness in his neck seeped out. Encouraged, he let his mind take him to those moments on the back steps when he'd held her hair in his fingers, letting that swath of gold glide over his flesh. He allowed an imaginary vision to follow the memory: gilt and earth hair glazing breasts shaped like half moons, her pale eyes turning quicksilver with need. He imagined kissing her, and wondered if it would be a surprise, or if she'd seen the curiosity and growing attraction in his eyes.

A pleasant lassitude spread through him, building a defense against stabbing thoughts of Josefina. Pleasant to think of a woman's body, the give of a breast, the heat of her thighs, the long, lazy ways he liked to make love. So much better than worry, he thought, leaning his head back, his fingers idly caressing the cat's back. So much better to think of kisses, and it had been a very long time since he'd allowed himself the luxury. He closed his eyes. Molly's mouth. Yes. Molly's breasts.

Molly found Alejandro asleep on the couch. She bent down, afraid she would lose her nerve if she delayed, and put her hand on his shoulder. "Alejandro."

He stirred, turning his head, and opening those dark liquid eyes. Sleep made his lids heavy, and he blinked once, then stretched a hand up to her face. "Saint Molly," he murmured, a soberness lying across his forehead as he looked up at her. His lashes, so extravagant, gave his eyes a kind of starriness. His thumb moved, and Molly, afraid he was going to caress her mouth, grabbed his wrist.

It didn't stop him. With the pad of his thumb, he touched her lower lip, brushing over the flesh lightly. So lightly it was like a breath, and yet she felt the radiating reaction in the tiny hairs that rose on her body, down her nape, across her shoulders, down to her breasts and the front of her thighs. She wanted to open her lips a little, touch her tongue to the tip of his thumb, but only knelt there next to him, feeling his hand on her face, her lip, and recognized that she'd never felt this level of desire for a man in her life.

He blinked, slowly, and his hand slid down her neck. "You're so beautiful," he murmured. "So alone."

Lonely.

Desire evaporated in the heat of humiliation and she turned her head away, her mouth tight, taking his wrist and putting his hand back on his own body. "You're not awake," she said briskly. "Wake up, Alejandro. This is important."

"I am awake," he said. But then her tone seemed to penetrate, and he frowned. "What is it?" He straightened too fast and she heard him grunt. His hands flew to his ribs, and Molly, loath as she was to touch him, put a hand against his back to ease him up.

"What did you learn?" he said harshly.

"It's good news," she said. "Josefina is okay."

He lifted his head and blinked at her. "What did you say?"

She smiled. "Josefina is found. They brought her to the hospital. She's sick, but I told her you were okay, too." Aware of the places she still touched him, her palm to his back, her knee against his thigh, she shifted to the chair near his knees. "But she's found."

An exhalation gusted from him, a sound of profound relief. He closed his eyes, uttering a soft prayer of thanks. To her surprise, he reached for Molly's hand. In the fierce grip of his fingers, she felt the force of his emotion. After a moment, he said, "Now you will not worry about your brother. We will go soon, and he will not know."

Molly bowed her head. Released his hand to give herself some distance. "It isn't that easy, Alejandro."

"Why? What do you mean?"

"I told you she is sick. You knew a little of that— you took her to the Health Services clinic, right? And they gave you inhalers."

He frowned. "Yes, they said she had the asthma."

"It's not asthma. We aren't sure yet, but it looks like tuberculosis." She shook her head and spilled the rest very quickly. "The tests aren't back yet, but I'm going to tell you, it *is* TB, and it's serious, and she will have to be in the hospital for a while.''

He touched her hand, once, lightly. ''Molly, go slower, eh?''

''Sorry.'' But she took another big breath to fuel the rest of the words coming out of her now. ''I thought and thought about this, and I don't know what you'll think, but there are no real answers, Alejandro. Not without lying.'' She could not bear to sit there and tell him the rest of the plan, so she jumped up and paced to the middle of the room, turned and folded her arms across her chest.

''This is my suggestion—we could tell everyone we met before and fell madly in love and we're going to get married and then Josefina can get her medicine and you can get tested without getting deported, and maybe you can find some real work around here because it takes eighteen months for her to take all the medicine.''

He went very still, his face completely unreadable. ''Say that again. Very slowly. I do not want to misunderstand.''

Feeling a painful heat in her face, Molly took a breath. ''If we do a wedding, pretending to be in love, Josefina can be treated for her illness.'' She lifted a shoulder. ''It won't have to be for long. Once your citizenship is established, we can divorce.''

He looked away for a moment, and his hair fell forward, hiding his expression. Molly pressed her lips together, letting her offer settle, wondering if she'd offended him. ''It's not only for you,'' she added. ''The whole town is going to find out that Molly Sheffield, the deputy sheriff's sister, was aiding and abetting a fugitive. I dispensed antibiotics and provided medical care for which I'm not licensed.''

When he still was silent, she shook her head. "Okay," she said breathily. "You're right, it was a silly idea. I didn't mean to offend you."

He raised his head. "Offend me?"

Her hands fluttered, touched her breast, her face. She clasped them together in front of her. "Yes, make you mad."

Alejandro stood, very straight. Lean, too, and much taller than she. Graveness marked his mouth. "I did not mean I don't know the word. I know *offend*." He touched her shoulder lightly. "I also know honor."

Stiffly, Molly looked up at him, unable to hide the tears of humiliation in her eyes or the flush of embarrassment in her face. As if he saw it, he lifted his hands and touched the fingertips to her cheeks. In her own defense, she began, "You must think—"

"I think you are kind." He laughed a little. "I think you are Mother Teresa, eh? It seems so." He lowered his hands to her arms. "If you do this thing for my niece and I, I will do anything to repay you. Fix your house. Plant your fields. Drive your car. Whatever you ask, that thing I will do."

His eyes glowed. His grip on her arms was loose, but firm. Intent somehow. She let go of a shaky breath. "Then we have a deal." Again she bit her lip. "There is one more thing."

He stepped back as she moved away, crossing her arms. "Everyone knows me here. The only way this will work is if we pretend that I've been seeing you since you arrived. We have to pretend that we fell in love."

A wicked, wicked grin, one that showed that half moon of dazzling teeth, illuminated his face. He lifted one black, arched eyebrow. "In love, eh?"

Abruptly, she sank to a chair and covered her face. "Oh, this is so weird. I swear I'm not playing a game with you, okay? I'm a widow and I have been for a long time, so I'm not just trying to…get your attention." She dropped her hands. "I really loved my husband. I still miss him. This is just an act."

He swallowed the smile. "I understand, Molly. We pretend only."

"Right. Okay, but this is the weird part—they have to believe us. Or everything will be worse. A lot worse. My brother, especially. Can you pretend to be wildly in love?"

He inclined his head, and she felt his gaze slide over her hair, touch her breasts, her hands. Mockingly, he pursed his lips, as if considering, and tsked. Sighing heavily, he said, "Well, I will try."

She gave him a faint smile. "You're teasing me."

He laughed, and it occurred to her that she had not heard the sound before. It rolled from his chest, as welcome as a desert rain. He moved close and held out a hand to her. "Come."

Warily, Molly accepted his hand and let him pull her to her feet. Her heart stuttered for a moment, as anticipation or fear or something rose in her chest.

Then he cupped her face in his palm and bent to kiss the other cheek. A wash of his hair touched her nose, and she caught her breath defensively against the wealth of scent that came with him, a scent unlike any she'd ever smelled, anywhere on the earth. It was his flesh, his hair, his honor. *"Gracias,"* he said quietly.

"You're welcome," she said, and pulled back. "Let's get this in motion now. You have to come to the hospital with me."

"To see Josefina?"

"Yes," she said. Squarely, she met his eyes. "And to show them we are in love."

"Ah." Again that new wickedness showed in his expression. "Should we...try to see if we can do it?"

"What do you mean?"

He stepped close, lifting his hands to her face. "Practice?"

Before she could protest, Alejandro bent again and pressed that beautiful mouth to hers.

His mouth.

She closed her eyes, letting everything she was flow to that place, putting every thought, every caution on hold so that she could indulge the purely physical pleasure of kissing Alejandro.

There was the scent, first of all. She knew there had never been a man who smelled this good. And there was the sound, a soft sound of air moving through their lungs.

But mostly, there was touch. His magnificent mouth, wide enough, and full enough for a truly sensual kind of kiss that needed no tongue, only the slight, explorative movements of flesh against charged flesh, a slide, a press, a purse, a release.

Have mercy. She made a soft sound and moved a little closer, feeling now things just beyond the field of actual touch—the suggestion of his chest very close to her breasts, the knowledge of his belly and sex so very close to her own.

As if her mouth surprised him, he lifted his head and their eyes met for one electric moment of dazzlement and pleasure and surprise, then he bent again, this time with more intent, his hand sliding from her face to the back of her head, the fingers long against her scalp, bracing her as he tilted his head and fitted their mouths more closely together. There was no fumble, no misstep, only a surprisingly harmonious meeting.

Somehow, she found her hands on his chest, not to push him away, but to steady herself so that she could tilt her head, part her lips a little. And yet, still, even though she tasted the warmth of his breath, sensed the moistness of his tongue beyond his barely open lips, he restrained himself. He only kissed her lips, delicately, first the lower, then the upper, then a corner. Soft kisses, whispers, a slight sweep of tongue over her lower lip, a sweep that sent a rocket of sensation through her body.

She tugged at his hand. "Alejandro," she said softly, and opened her eyes. "Please...I..."

He dropped his hands, stepped away. "Good practice, no?"

She nodded, resisted the urge to put her hand to her tingling lips. "Yes." She swallowed.

Suddenly, the enormity of her every action since this man had landed—literally—on her property sunk in, and she found herself disoriented. Lost. Shaky. Scared. "We'll go to the hospital in a couple of hours. I think...uh...I need to get a few hours of sleep." She backed away. "Josefina will sleep till morning."

"Molly, I did not mean—"

"It isn't you." She managed a very small smile. "I'm just tired."

He nodded, frowning. "Sleep then. I will make some coffee for you when you wake up, no?"

Molly blinked. "Okay."

Chapter 7

Alone in her bedroom, Molly closed the door and shed her clothes hastily, as if they contained the poison that was corrupting her blood. Shrugging into a thick robe, she gathered clean underwear and toiletries, and went to the bathroom for a shower, moving furtively through the hall, her head down, afraid to look up and see him and—

What? Throw herself on his mercy? Her face flamed as she imagined herself begging him to make love to her. Now. Any way he liked. Just so she could shed her clothes and put her whole self against his nakedness.

What was it about him, anyway, that inflamed her so intensely? She wasn't a woman given to such lustful imaginings. She just...didn't do it. Sex had been a pleasurable discovery, and one she enjoyed, but it was like gardening or painting—satisfying but not electrifying.

But from the moment she'd first seen Alejandro's face, she'd been aflame.

In the bathroom, she locked the door, glared at herself and said, "Don't you dare make a fool of yourself, Molly."

She turned the water on. Hot. Hot hot hot. Steam curled up the walls, misted the line of small windows where greenery lived, enveloped her in its embrace, and somehow, it helped.

Alejandro had put his finger on the problem last night. She was lonely. Not only that, she was living in a lonely place, a place she'd bought as a newlywed, and worked on with her husband. She had believed the rooms would one day be filled with the laughter of children.

Instead, she lived here alone, outside of town, where she couldn't even see a neighbor's lamp burning in the night.

She put her hand flat against the varnished pine wall Tim had been so proud of, and she remembered his hand—that white, freckled, golden-furred hand—resting there, too. As if making up for the months in which she had finally begun to miss him less, wave after wave of tactile, physical memory assailed her. His laughter in her ear. His bony feet. His thick blond hair and sturdy shoulders. The little paunch he put on in the winter.

It seemed odd to her, suddenly, that she had begun to believe that her penance was over. She had managed to walk upright through her grief, had not fallen to drink or depression or any of the other pitfalls that might have lessened her virtue in grieving.

What, exactly, had she hoped to gain in that virtue? The answer was inexplicable and yet perfectly clear in terms of emotional logic: she had, somewhere in her, expected to get him *back*. She showed the universe she could be tested without cracking, and she'd been waiting, with half-held breath, for the universe to give her back her husband.

The recognition hit her like a blow.

Kissing Alejandro had brought home the futility of that secret, illogical wish. If her husband was coming back, she wouldn't betray him by lusting after another man. She wouldn't have allowed a kiss.

She wouldn't have suggested a green-card wedding, either. With a sense of tearing, she found herself forced to let go, to face the fact that, no matter how virtuous she'd been, Tim was never, ever going to come back.

With a cry, she sank to the bathroom floor and wept. Not tiny baby tears. Great, gulping, engulfing sobs. Her exhaustion and the sudden events of the past few days had made her vulnerable, but she recognized that was only the trigger. Seeing Tim's clothes on Alejandro, touching him, feeling again that richness of life in her arousal, her attraction, had brought home how very gone her husband was.

Gone.

She wept.

Alejandro let Molly retreat, recognizing the unsettling trueness of that kiss—a kiss that had begun as a way to lighten the tension between them, make her smile, and had become...something else.

He was in the kitchen, making coffee for himself, when he heard the sobs. The sound drew him, and he made his way down the hall in concern. He knew this sound. It was grief—the kind that stole over a person and sucked out the breath, nearly stopped the heart.

He'd known it only twice in his life, at the death of his parents and upon the death of his sister.

Standing outside the bathroom door, he hesitated. The shower was running and maybe she had hoped that it would drown the sound of her sorrow. And yet it had not. He could not bear to think of her so very, very sad and alone after all she'd given him and Josefina. He knocked, firmly, so she would hear over the shower. *"Señora?"*

A beat of silence, one broken by a strangled sound. "I'm okay."

"No, no." He jiggled the door handle, to let her know he meant to come in. "You do not need to be so alone when I am here to help you."

"I'm okay," she repeated.

He thought for a moment, and leaned against the door. "Saint Molly, will you let me give back just this one thing? *Por favor?"*

Silence. Then the door opened, and she stood there looking small and impossibly frail in an oversize robe, her hair loose on her shoulders, her face ravaged and unbeautiful in grief. Her eyes burned an unholy color of silver in the midst of the red of weeping, and Alejandro did exactly what came to him: he moved forward, closed the door to prevent the heat and damp of the steam from leaving the room and enfolded her in his arms. He held her tightly, without hesitation, putting a hand on her head to encourage her to lie it in the cradle of his shoulder. She was stiff for a moment, resisting, then something broke free and she gripped him, buried her face, and he felt her shoulders shake. "It's been four years," she moaned. "How can it still hurt like this, all at once, so I can't breathe?"

"It does, that's all." His balance was precarious, and

he braced himself against the door, stroking her hair, stroking, stroking.

"He's not coming back. Not ever."

"No," he said quietly. The shower ran and ran, and the steam was so thick in the room that his face was wet in moments. "But he *was* here. He lived. In these rooms, no?" He rubbed his cheek on her hair, not out of longing, but out of need to comfort. "He wore this shirt. He loved you, and you loved him."

She nodded, and more tears fell, a river of them, but these were somehow richer, less stricken.

"You will not forget him, Saint Molly. And now I will know him, too, by knowing you. Any man you loved so well must have been very fine."

"He was." The words came out strangled, but he felt the difference in her. Moving gently, he settled her on the toilet and reached for the washcloth. He ran cold water on it and started to kneel before the assorted pains in him stopped that action.

Instead, he bent, putting one hand on her shoulder to brace himself a little, and used the other to blot her hot, swollen face. She closed her eyes with a sigh and let him press the cold cloth to her eyelids. "Thank you."

"If my kiss made that come, I am sorry, Molly."

She raised her face, put a hand to his wrist. "It was just that it made me remember. It wasn't you."

And with a fierceness that surprised him, he suddenly wanted to kiss her with all the passion that lived in him. Wanted to tangle with her in a way that bruised and healed them both. It swelled in him, swift and biting, this lust, and shocked him enough that he stepped back. "The water will be cold," he said, and put the washcloth in her hand.

* * *

After her shower, Molly fell into bed and slept for nearly four hours. It was the sleep of the dead, and she felt cleansed when she awakened. Her mind was sharp and clear as she dressed and drank some of Alejandro's extraordinary coffee. "You really will have to show me how to make this," she said, standing at the sink in the sunshine.

She had brought him fresh clothing, more things that had belonged to Tim, right down to the boxer shorts. He looked troubled when she carried them out of the bedroom. "Are you sure, *señora?* I do not wish to cause you more pain."

"He would kill me if I let those clothes sit there when someone could get some use out of them," she said briskly, and meant it.

They did not, Molly admitted now, fit him particularly well. Alejandro was a little taller and a good twenty pounds lighter than Tim had been, so the sleeves and jeans were the smallest bit too short, and everything was baggy. He obviously knew this, too, for he plucked restlessly at the shirt collar, tried to smooth the button placket as if to make it fit better. "Don't worry about it," Molly said now. "We'll get some more clothes for you."

He scowled. "No. I cannot allow that."

"How about if I write it down, keep an account? Will that make you feel better?"

He considered. The angle of cheekbone to eyebrow to chin remained impassive, but he could not halt the movements of that wide, mobile mouth, which finally pursed into an expression of agreement. "*Sí.* I can make money in only a week or two. Then I can repay you."

"Fair enough."

Parked outside the hospital a little while later, Molly made a move to open the door. He stopped her. "Are you certain you wish to do this?"

She did not even hesitate. "Yes."

"Will they believe you are in love with such a man?"

"Such a man." Even in the ill-fitting clothes, he was a sight for starved women's eyes—the black-licorice hair, neatly combed away from his face to fall around his collar in thick waves, the liquid dark eyes in a face of striking angles, the sensual mouth. "Oh, yes, Alejandro. They will believe."

"And all men could see why I would find passion for such a woman," he said lightly, but the words touched her. "Come, then. I wish to see my niece."

Leaning on a cane she'd brought to him from the hospital, he rounded the car and took her hand, raising his eyebrows a little as he did so. "For courage."

And oddly, it did lend her courage to have her hand firmly clasped in his as they walked, a promise of kept secrets.

The halls were quiet as they entered—it was just past nine, and there had evidently been no more new emergencies through the night. Molly had timed their arrival so that they would not miss Cathy, her supervisor, and she found her at the nurses' station, one hand in her already mussed hair as she scribbled notes on an insurance form.

"Cathy," Molly said quietly.

The woman looked up, blinking, and then blinked again as she took in the fact that Molly was not alone.

"This is Alejandro Sosa," Molly said. "He is the uncle of the little girl Wiley brought in last night." She took a breath, and as if he felt her nervousness, Alejandro tightened his fingers around hers. "He is also my fiancé."

Clearly, Cathy could not take it in. "Fiancé? As in getting married to?"

"Yes." On the spur of the moment, she made up a story. "I—we—had planned to go through proper channels, but circumstances have forced us to move up the date."

Cathy looked from Molly to Alejandro, then stood up and held out her hand. "I'm so happy to meet you."

"Thank you."

"Keep it under your hat for a little while, huh?" Molly asked. "I'm going to see my brother after we are finished here. I'd rather he heard the news from me."

Cathy raised her eyebrows. "That should go over well."

"Oh, yeah." Molly shrugged. "I think we need to see Josefina now. Have any of the tests come back?"

Cathy rounded the desk to accompany them, and as they walked down the hall to the little girl's room, she said, "The labs will take a few days, but based on the X rays, it's undoubtedly TB."

No surprise, but Molly squeezed Alejandro's hand, sparing a look at him. His mouth was set in a line.

Outside the room, Cathy provided them with face masks. "Standard procedure," she explained to Alejandro.

He nodded and tied the mask around his face. Cathy pushed open the door, and Alejandro winked at Molly. "Do I look like a desperado?"

She grinned. "Dangerous."

Josefina turned her head as they came in, and when

she saw who it was, she cried out in almost painful recognition, "Tío!"

Alejandro was across the room and hugging her before Molly could blink. Until now, the connection between these two had been purely academic, a fact without substance. Now, the girl wept in sobbing hiccups, and Alejandro hugged her gently, kissing her head, murmuring to her in Spanish. The words were unclear to Molly, but the gist was clear, *Everything is okay.*

It took a few minutes but at last Alejandro settled his niece on the pillows, tugged the blankets over her and parked his hand on her forehead. "You are very sick, *hija.* Did they tell you?"

"Molly told me." The child pointed to her and Molly went around to the other side of the bed, taking her hand. "Last night."

"Right." Their eyes met. "We talked."

"Tío," she said, and spoke quickly, excitedly, in Spanish. Alejandro stopped her after a moment, saying, "We must speak English, so our Molly can hear, too." He looked at Molly. "She told me she spent her money well. Made it last for three meals, and she found a way to get a blanket so she would not be cold at night." With a gentle smile, he turned to Josefina and added, "I am very proud of you."

Cathy waved at Molly, and exited. Molly let go of a sigh of relief. "So far, so good."

Alejandro glanced over his shoulder. "Keep watch while I tell Josefina what we're going to do."

They went shopping at a brightly lit department store when they left the hospital. Alejandro was conscious of the money he was spending, and chose only two pairs of jeans that fit him, and three shirts, all long-sleeved. One had snaps on the pointed pockets, but Molly's amused expression made him hesitate. "Is this not right?"

"If you want it to be. Only old men wear those shirts now, though."

"Ah." He grinned and gestured toward the rack. "Then you choose for me. Proper American clothes."

She flipped through the multicolored cottons on their hangers, using that brisk, decisive gesture women employed. *Clack, clack, clack* as the colors or patterns were dismissed. She pulled one out, a dark shade of blue, and held it up to him, then rejected it. *Clack. Clack, clack.* Another, this one of some soft fabric he didn't know how to name, in a shade of deep turquoise. She held it up and smiled. "They'll really swoon over you in this."

They? he wondered, smiling as she narrowed her eyes. Or her? He put on the shirt in the men's room before they left, and was pleased at the sudden deepening of the silver in her eyes.

All day, he had been trying to keep his thoughts away from the kiss that had lingered on his nerves for hours afterward, away from the way she had felt in his arms when she wept for her lost husband—ah, so deep a love she'd found!—away from that swift, fierce wish to make love to her.

She did not make it easy. He liked the feel of her hand in his, small and strong. He liked her throaty laughter and the flash of her eyes. As they moved toward the car to go to see her brother, he liked the way her breasts bounced slightly beneath her shirt.

And he was shamed by his desire. What did he have to offer her? In his own country, he had been modestly successful, enough that he had been considering the possibility of marriage when his sister died.

Here, he had nothing. Less than nothing—no home, no family ties, no money or way of procuring it legally. On this bright October day, those facts stung his pride, but also reminded him that he could not allow himself the indulgence of desire.

It was wrong for another reason. She was not ready for a man yet. Not any man who was not her husband. Though he sometimes saw appreciation in her pale eyes, her heart belonged still to her lost husband.

One day Alejandro would repay her extraordinary kindness. He vowed it to himself, a sacred promise. In the meantime, he would do what he could to ease her worry over the trouble she might face over this situation.

As they drove through a settled town neighborhood of small, well-tended houses, her nervousness increased. He saw it in the way she tightened her hands on the steering wheel, leaning forward as if by peering through the windshield hard enough she would be able to tell the future.

"You are worried about your brother, no?"

She glanced at him. "Yes."

"Tell me what I should know of him."

"Josh is a good man," she said. "But we lost our parents in a car accident when he was sixteen, and it affected him badly. He wants to make sure nothing bad ever happens again, and he thinks he can make that happen by controlling everything."

Alejandro nodded. "I see."

"That's not all of it." She took a breath. "Don't ask me where this came from, but he sees it as his sacred duty to scour the country free of 'aliens.'" She pulled the car up in front of a tiny yellow house with an even smaller square of lawn. Everything about the place was almost painfully meticulous, from the swept walk to the garden hoses rolled up on a caddy. "If he even suspects that we're not really in love, he'll make it his personal quest to deport you."

He frowned. "Is this wise, then, Molly?"

She turned off the engine, staring at the house for a long moment. "No. It really isn't. But it's the only chance you have."

A wave of gratitude washed over him, and he bent close, putting a hand on her face. "He will never doubt, not for one moment, that I am in love with you."

"There he is," she whispered urgently. "Kiss me like you really mean it."

That he could do. He closed the small space between them and cupped her chin, lifting her face to his, and kissed her. In this, he could use his desire. And in his desire, he was not so careful, so restrained as he'd been last night. He coaxed her lips apart with his tongue, and felt a burst of heat when their tongues touched, danced, circled. Her hands came around his neck, her fingers sliding into his hair, and then she tilted her head, as if in genuine heat, to urge him closer. Alejandro met the deepening with a shock of pleasure. Their tongues touched, tip to tip, then skittered away, and came back again to slide together, slide apart, meet again.

He felt his breath come more quickly, felt the small, eager leaps of his sex as it wakened, and he told himself it was enough, this kiss looked good enough for her brother.

But she showed no sign of wishing to stop, and Alejandro let himself go entirely, swirling, tasting, plucking. He suckled her lower lip for a brief second and heard her cry out in surprise and pleasure, so he did it again, putting his tongue into it. She softened in reaction, and one breast pressed lightly into his chest.

A rap at the car door made them break apart, but neither turned immediately toward the sound. She gazed up at him, her silvery eyes almost too bright to look upon. With his thumb, he brushed moisture from her lip, still holding her gaze.

Then, as if they could speak without speaking, they turned together toward the man standing outside the car in a khaki sheriff's uniform, hands on his hips.

"For the love of Mike, Molly, get out of there and stop making out like a teenager."

Molly gave Alejandro a wicked little grin over her shoulder and pushed open her door. Alejandro stepped out on the passenger side, leaning heavily on his cane. The man in uniform planted his lean but sturdy body in the path and glared at him, his gaze flickering with distaste from the top of his head to his feet. "Who is this?"

"Alejandro Sosa." She paused to let that sink in, then, "He is my fiancé." Molly joined Alejandro and slid her hand into his. "Alejandro, this is my brother, Josh."

Alejandro held out his hand, knowing it would be ignored. "How do you do?"

"What the hell is this, Molly?"

"Let's go inside, Josh. I want Lynette to meet him, too, and there's no point in your standing out here yelling at me for all the neighbors to hear."

Josh glared at Alejandro. Alejandro had seen the look before, a hundred times, a thousand. It was an expression that said the wearer knew all there was to

know of his kind. In most cases, the gaze was one of
distaste, and perhaps a little fear. But in Molly's
brother's eyes, Alejandro glimpsed a much more dangerous emotion than distaste. It was hate.

Alejandro lifted his chin and let the pride of five
hundred years of culture fill him. In him ran the blood
of the Aztecs and the conquistadores, who had done as
much damage as good, but had been first even on this
land under their feet. What his education had given
him—pride in his language and his people—could not
be stolen by the evil eye of a man who was afraid.

"Please," Molly said again, more urgently.

Abruptly, Josh gave up his aggressive stance and
spun toward the house. Molly looked up at Alejandro,
and he glimpsed the worry in her face. He held out his
hand, smiling wryly. "He will not hurt you."

"Not intentionally," Molly said bleakly, but she accepted his hand and they walked to the house.

Inside, the usual chaos greeted them. Toys were
strewn in no particular trail through the living room—
trucks, plastic blocks, doll clothes.

Josh cursed as he made his way through the mine-
field. "Lynette!" he roared, "make these kids pick up
their stuff!"

Lynette came out of the kitchen, drying her hands
on a towel. "Don't be such a grouch, honey!" Only
then did she spy Molly and Alejandro, who hung back
a little. Her eyes widened.

Molly knew she had to hit exactly the right notes in
front of her friend. They had been best friends since
kindergarten. For a while last night, she had even considered telling Lynette the truth, but realized in time
that the confession would put Lynette in a difficult po-

sition. So, although it pained her to lie to her friend, Molly intended to convince Lynette she was besotted.

To that end, she looked up at Alejandro and smiled, and tugged his hand. "This is my best friend, Lynette, Alejandro."

Josh snorted. "They're engaged," he said in a nasty singsong.

"What?" Lynette's face was a study in bewilderment. First shock, then a sliding glance to Alejandro, which turned her expression to one of consideration, then a glance at her husband, before she looked back to Molly with amazement.

"Oh my God," she finally said, and sailed—through some uncanny mother instinct—over the toys and into Molly's arms. "How wonderful!" she screeched, her arms a vise.

Then, in one of the gestures that had made her Molly's best friend for all of life, she turned to Alejandro and hugged him, too. "Welcome to the family!" she cried. "I'm amazed, but I'm so happy for you! I think I have some champagne somewhere. Come in the kitchen and let's have a toast."

She led the way, and shooed the children out of the kitchen. "Go pick up your toys, guys, and you can come back and take a peek at your new uncle."

Both children dropped their mouths. "New uncle?"

"Yep, right there in front of you." She shooed them with her fingers. "Go pick up the toys first. Pronto, pronto." She glanced up and gave Alejandro an abashed expression. "Sorry! I wasn't making fun of you, I promise. I mean, you are Mexican, aren't you? Oh, I'm only making this worse!"

Alejandro laughed, that low, sexy sound, and shook

Play the "LAS VEGAS" Game
and get
3 FREE GIFTS!

FREE GIFTS!

FREE GIFTS!

1. Pull back all 3 tabs on the card at right. Then check the claim chart to see what we have for you — 2 FREE BOOKS and a gift — ALL YOURS! ALL FREE!

2. Send back this card and you'll receive brand-new Silhouette Intimate Moments® novels. These books have a cover price of $4.25 each in the U.S. and $4.75 each in Canada, but they are yours to keep absolutely free.

3. There's no catch. You're under no obligation to buy anything. We charge nothing — ZERO — for your first shipment. And you don't have to make any minimum number of purchases — not even one!

4. The fact is thousands of readers enjoy receiving books by mail from the Silhouette Reader Service™. They like the convenience of home delivery... they like getting the best new novels BEFORE they're available in stores... and they love our discount prices!

5. We hope that after receiving your free books you'll want to remain a subscriber. But the choice is yours — to continue or cancel, any time at all! So why not take us up on our invitation, with no risk of any kind. You'll be glad you did!

Yours Free!

FREE!
No Obligation to Buy!
No Purchase Necessary!

Play the

"LAS VEGAS" Game

> **PEEL BACK HERE ▶**
> **PEEL BACK HERE ▶**
> **PEEL BACK HERE ▶**

YES! I have pulled back the 3 tabs. Please send me all the free Silhouette Intimate Moments® books and the gift for which I qualify. I understand that I am under no obligation to purchase any books, as explained on the back and opposite page.

345 SDL CT4L
　　　　　　　　　　　　　　　　　　　245 SDL CT4E

Name	(Please Print Clearly)	
Address		Apt.
City	State/Prov.	Zip/Postal Code

GET 2 FREE BOOKS & A FREE MYSTERY GIFT!

GET 2 FREE BOOKS!

GET 1 FREE BOOK!

TRY AGAIN!

Offer limited to one per household and not valid to current Silhouette Intimate Moments® subscribers. All orders subject to approval.

(S-IM-11/99)

PRINTED IN U.S.A.

If offer card is missing write to: Silhouette Reader Service, 3010 Walden Ave., P.O. Box 1867, Buffalo, NY 14240-1867

BUSINESS REPLY MAIL
FIRST-CLASS MAIL   PERMIT NO. 717   BUFFALO, NY

POSTAGE WILL BE PAID BY ADDRESSEE

SILHOUETTE READER SERVICE
3010 WALDEN AVE
PO BOX 1867
BUFFALO NY 14240-9952

NO POSTAGE
NECESSARY
IF MAILED
IN THE
UNITED STATES

his head. "It would be a mean man who was offended with you."

"Thank you. Sit down." She swept the children's dishes from the table.

Through it all, Molly kept her attention on her brother. He flung himself against the counter, arms crossed, and waited for everything to settle, his eyes hard on Molly. "No way," he said at last. "This is just bull—"

"Josh," Lynette warned.

"Bullcrap," he said instead. "I don't believe this is some big love match, Molly Sheffield. How long have you known him?"

Alejandro spoke. "It has not been long, it is true. But time is sometimes not needed."

"How long?"

Molly looked at Alejandro, urging him silently to field this one. She had no idea when he'd arrived at Wiley Farms. He acknowledged her urgency with a nod. "I came here only three weeks ago."

Josh rolled his eyes. "Molly, I want to talk to you. Alone."

Alejandro half rose, but Molly shook her head silently. She'd known how hard this part would be, and with Josh in his current temper, she didn't particularly want to subject Alejandro to any more of his raving.

Josh strode into his bedroom and closed the door. In a low, tight voice, he said, "What the hell do you think you're doing, Moll?"

As calmly as possible, Molly replied, "I knew this wouldn't be easy for you."

"You're damned right." He paced toward the window, then back. "How could you?"

"How could I what? Fall in love? It happens all the time."

"He's a friggin' alien! I can't believe you have anything in common enough to fall in love." He licked his bottom lip, his eyes narrowing. "I knew there was something wrong that night you bought me a steak at the café. Like you had a guilty conscience."

"Come on, Josh. I've done it a hundred times. It gives me pleasure to help you sometimes. I don't have to have an ulterior motive."

"Not always. But you were weird that night. Asking about the kid—I suppose it's the little girl they found on Wiley's land."

She nodded. A knot of discomfort made her stomach ache. She didn't like to lie, and it seemed she'd done little else the past few days.

But was lying to save someone's life really a sin? In this case, she felt justified, though her brother would certainly disagree. The thought made her utter a swift prayer: God, please never let him find out the truth!

"From what I hear, she's pretty sick," he said. "Same age as Rochelle. Makes me sad to think of her out there for two days, scared and alone."

"Me, too, Josh. We were both worried to death about her. And she is very sick. She has TB."

He shook his head. Some of the anger drained from his face and softened his shoulders. "Moll, I know how you are. I can see why you'd take in some lost kid, why you'd want to help these two. But don't you see? If you do, you give every other illegal for two thousand miles an excuse to keep trying."

She sighed. "Josh—"

"Don't say it, Molly. I don't want you to have to lie to me anymore. Let's just let it stand—you're marrying this guy to help his little girl, and we both know it.'' His jaw went hard. ''If I can prove it, I'll deport him so fast you won't even know what happened.''

Anger burst in Molly. ''You go ahead and try. I'm in love with him and I'm going to marry him!'' She sighed. ''Can't you just be happy for me, Josh? I've been so damned lonely since Tim died.''

''I know. But what has this guy got to offer you? Some poor Mexican illegal with a third-grade education?''

She scowled, hearing in his assumptions a reflection of her own early expectations. Shame touched her again. ''Don't be so quick to jump to conclusions about who he is.''

He rolled his eyes. ''I've seen enough of these guys that I don't have to make assumptions. I deal with them, remember?''

''Who do you deal with, Josh? Do you know anything about them? Have you ever had a conversation with even one of those guys? About their lives, about their educations, about their reasons for being here?''

''No! And I don't care. They don't belong here. They're making it hard on the rest of us. I pay my taxes and pay my insurance and as far as I'm concerned, they're taking money directly out of my pocket!''

''Josh—''

''No, I don't want to hear it. We'll never agree on this.''

A pang of separation struck her. If she chose Alejandro, she was going to lose her brother. How could she make that kind of choice?

''Can't you just give him a chance? He's not who you think he is. He's an honorable man, Josh.''

He only shook his head. "When are you going to do the deed?"

Molly hadn't thought that far ahead. Recklessly, she said, "Saturday. Please come."

"Not a chance."

Staring at his sullen, closed face, Molly knew she had no choice. "I'm sorry," she said. "I'll miss you."

Chapter 8

Alejandro was drained by the time they went back out to the car. Molly saw it in the paleness of his jaw and the grim set of his mouth, but he asked if they could go by Wiley Farms. He had money waiting there, and his guitar and some of his things. Wiley's wife told them that he'd taken the little dog to the vet. She chuckled. "Ugliest little mutt you ever saw, but Jim's been treating him like a king."

"Good." The dog could stay here, pampered, until Josefina was out of the hospital. Molly suspected Leo would not be happy about a dog. Any dog.

A ranch hand took them down to the bunkhouse, and unlocked a storeroom. There were no clothes, none of Alejandro's or Josefina's—"we give 'em all to the Salvation Army. No point in keepin' 'em"—but the guitar was tucked against the wall, a long woven strap attached to the neck. The check was delivered without a quibble.

Back at the house, Alejandro muttered a blindly exhausted apology and collapsed in his bed. Molly fetched more antibiotics and some ibuprofen, and roused him enough to insist he swallow the pills, but he was down for the count after that.

In a way, it was a relief. Not to think about him. Not to gauge her actions by where he was in her house, but simply move around as she always had before he came.

As she would do when he left. Humming softly to herself, she made a pizza for dinner and some iced tea and carried them outside to the patio. It seemed as if it should be later, after all that had transpired today, but the sun was at its most golden, hanging over the mountains like the magic ball of some oracle, and the rays were warm.

Leo came out to beg for scraps and she fed him tiny pieces of cheese and let him chase a long stalk of grass she swished along the tiles.

And the whole time she made dinner, the whole while she played with her cat, what she itched to do was call Lynette and pour everything out to her. It was the first time in her life that she had not been free to do that—she couldn't remember going through anything, even something like picking out a dress for a dance, without using Lynette as a sounding board.

The only other time Molly could remember that she and Lynette had not discussed every little detail of life was when Lynette had come home from a summer trip and had fallen—head over heels—for Josh. Josh was younger, for one thing, and the younger brother of her very best friend, and they were both very young when it happened—not even twenty.

But true love it had been, and after six months, Lynette had called and spilled all those days of silence in a phone call that lasted four hours.

The trouble now was Josh, too. It was damned inconvenient to have your brother marry your best friend, Molly thought.

And yet…would she really have spoken of this, anyway? Maybe not.

Finished with her supper, and unable to call Lynette, Molly found herself admiring the long sharp shapes of tree branches against the changing sky, and went inside to get her paints and enormous—and expensive!—watercolor tablet. She didn't bother with an easel, but propped the tablet against a chair and spent a quiet hour capturing the light, the shapes, the shadows, the colors, and didn't think at all.

Sometime after dark, Alejandro wandered out, stiff and still very sore, but also very, very hungry. Flickering blue light led him to the living room, where Molly sat curled on the couch like a girl, her feet tucked under her. She didn't see him immediately, and he paused in the darkness of the hall, struck by the ordinariness of the scene—the woman in an oversize shirt and tights or something, mesmerized by something on television, a bowl of popcorn at her side. Her hair was loosely tied in a knot at her nape, and wisps of it fell down her neck. He wanted to put his face against that place between her shoulder and neck, where it would smell warm.

He'd learned as a youth that sex was not an easy thing for him. It was too hard to lie with a woman and stay apart, to keep any portion of himself aloof from it. Twice, as a very young man, he had learned the lesson, that joining made him love, for right or wrong.

One more time, then, when he was older, though he was wiser, it happened again—afterward he thought of marriage, but his woman had simply wanted to make love. He had, being a man, wished for the same thing at first. But the feelings went too deep for him, and he could not bear the way she did not take their relationship seriously, and broke it off. She came to him sometimes after that, wanting his body, but she did not want what else went with it.

He was not a vain man, but he was not a fool, either. He'd seen, in his years, that women often wanted to lie with him. But not join, not heart to heart, as he did. So he learned to stay aloof from them in that way.

But kissing Molly had shattered those holds, that aloofness. He feared that kissing her was as dangerous as making love to someone else, that already he might be snared more deeply than he wished. As he watched her, he wanted to put his hands all over her, slowly, to fit his palms to the comma shape of her breasts, and uncover the curve of her belly. He thought he would like seeing her in the sunlight that way, seeing all of her and touching all of her, with no covering, no shadows, just Molly in her flesh and her long hair draped over her.

The cat raced out from some hidden place, startling Molly, and she jumped so violently that popcorn spilled all over the floor. The bowl clanged on the coffee table on the way down, and the cat jumped straight up in the air, three feet at least. Alejandro laughed out loud.

"You scared us both," she said, then held up a hand. "Watch him," she said, and he saw her shoulders shaking with laughter.

The cat crept up on the bowl, very, very slowly.

Molly moved her foot suddenly, and he skittered sideways, his eyes still focused on the upturned bowl as if it were an animal playing dead, one that would leap upon him at any second. When he was in reach, he carefully lifted a paw and then—*slam!*—banged it against the bowl. It wasn't quite stable and at the hit, rolled to its side. Leo jumped backward a solid two feet, and Molly dissolved into giggles.

Feeling sympathy, Alejandro bent far enough to scoop the animal up and hold him close, and murmured in Spanish, "Poor little thing. And she's laughing, eh?" Against his chest, Leonardo's fur felt luxurious, and the animal butted his hand against his chin for a minute, then, comforted plenty, demanded to be let down.

Molly was on her knees, picking up popcorn, still half smiling. Acting on impulse, Alejandro sank down beside her and started helping. He was still half-aroused, awareness prickling along the back of his neck, and in his keen observation of her, he didn't miss the slight shift of her body. Toward him, not away. When she thought he wasn't looking, her gaze went to his chest, and he could almost feel the brush of that lingering admiration, touching his belly, which was still very flat from his hard work, and his shoulders, and then away.

He wondered, picking up popcorn, what she would do if he did simply lean close and put his face against her neck. Would she bolt or respond? And which did he truly desire?

"I bet you're starving," she said. "There's pizza in the oven."

"Good." He inched a little closer. She picked up the bowl and put it on the table, and he moved again, until they were hip to hip. "Maybe," he said, leaning closer, "there is something I would like better, though, Molly."

She closed her eyes. That was all. Stayed exactly where she was and closed her eyes. And what was there to do, then? Alejandro leaned close and put his face against her neck, trailing the tip of his nose along her skin. A brush of hair tickled his cheek and he smiled, putting his forehead against her jaw. "I like your smell," he said.

"Alejandro," she said softly, "if you're doing this because you think it's a good way to repay me, it's okay. You don't have to."

He laughed and pulled back to look at her. "Is that what you think?"

A shrug. "Maybe. I mean, you must have women lined up for miles."

"Miles." He smiled, and lifted a hand, and this time he did not hesitate. "But let me tell you, they do not make me think in the ways I have been thinking of you today."

She raised her eyes. "What ways?"

For a moment, he did not know how to answer, and the sweet, lost hungriness in her eyes stole whatever he might have said. Instead, he found himself captured in the watercolor of her eyes.

They did not move, only sat, side to side, lost in a place that was born by the act of their joined gazes, a place that grew rapidly, excluding the rest of the world. Alejandro thought he could see through, beyond the surface of those irises, and he saw a life, a room where a girl had danced in her underwear before an oval mirror, a teen who stared up at the stars and wondered what if life existed on other worlds, a woman who had made love in this house to a man she had loved. He even thought he could see himself reflected back to him as a much better, stronger man than he was.

It gave him the strength to simply touch her face lightly with his fingertips, to lift his gaze away from the depth of those eyes to the part in her hair. He closed his eyes and pressed his mouth to the place where her hair met her forehead. Against her brow, he said, "I would kiss you until I died, I think. But that would be bad for you. Maybe bad for me, too."

Her hands lit on his shoulders, and she brushed her eye against his cheek. "Yes." Breaking away quickly, she rose. "I'll get you some of that pizza. How's that?"

Alejandro dropped his hands to his lap. "Yes, please."

Josh didn't even bother trying to sleep. When Lynette turned in, he sat up in the living room, idly channel-surfing through the four channels they actually got. No fifty-seven channels, here, no sirree. Cable was way out of the budget.

His gut burned, even through the antacids he'd been chewing for hours, and it was a burn of fury. Lynette had tried talking him down from his anger, but every time he thought he'd managed to put it aside, he saw his sister in her car, kissing that guy. He'd caught on one detail—a dark hand against his sister's pale face, and it burned in him.

On one level, he was appalled by his reaction. He'd never thought himself to be a racist. All his life, he'd had friends from other cultures. There weren't that many black people in the valley, but half the county was Latino, so a guy naturally made friends with them.

But the image burned in him nonetheless. That dark hand against her white face. That peasant hand. He hated to even hear him talk—that slurring Mexican accent.

And maybe, maybe, he could have gotten used to it—eventually—if he didn't feel in his gut that Molly was acting out of some noble instinct. Taking on this guy's problems because she was too nice and too trusting. He'd use her and throw her away, and Molly would have that lost, wounded look she'd only recently begun to lose. He couldn't stand to see her heart broken again.

Hypocrite!

The word burned across his forehead, and with a cry, Josh buried his face in his hands, trying to rub the brand away. He was so confused. Was he a racist at heart? Was that why he resented the aliens so much? Or was his anger reasonable?—he was struggling, so hard, to make ends meet, and they were taking money out of his pocket. Wasn't that a normal reaction?

He rubbed his forehead harder. There were no answers. Not right now. Maybe he needed to examine his heart to discover if he really was harboring some racist feelings. God knew his head, at least, wanted to believe it wasn't true, but if it was, he had to find out, so he didn't pass it on to his kids—or end up killing somebody out of anger.

He didn't know how to do it, but he'd think about it later.

The real issue was Molly marrying some stranger in some misguided rescue mission. That was what he had to stop, come hell or high water.

The rest could wait.

* * *

Molly and Alejandro spent the next morning with Josefina, who was weak and listless in a way that made Molly worry. The doctor simply said the child was exhausted and need more rest, so they left her to sleep, and set out to tackle the slightly awkward details of arranging the marriage.

After three stops, however, it was plain there was not a judge in the country who would agree to perform the ceremony, thanks to Josh's influence. Frustrated, Molly insisted they go ahead with the blood tests anyway, and while they were driving back, she had a brainstorm. "The details don't matter to you, do they?" she asked, pulling off the side of the road.

"No."

"I have an idea." She turned the car around and headed back to a dirt break off the two-lane highway. She grinned. "I'll bet you've never seen anything like what we're about to see."

A brace of trees marked the entrance, and they turned into what the locals, with no fondness, called "that hippie commune." In actuality, it was a loosely structured community of people with alternative values who'd banded together decades ago to grow organic food in a co-op. Sunshine Farms now boasted a bottom line well in the black, and with the addition of free-range meats, were on the way to making a serious fortune.

Some of those free-range chickens squawked and fluttered as she and Alejandro stepped out of the car, and he grinned, looking around himself. "Now, this is what I like."

A collection of houses in various styles dotted the hills, and animals in pens lowed or cackled or called. Beyond, for nearly as far as the eye could see, were fields, emptied now with the onset of winter, but obviously just harvested. A turquoise school bus, parked for twenty years, was painted with the exuberant, stylized sun logo of the farms. It served as the office, and a woman with a pageboy haircut and dressed in jeans stepped down from it. "Hi! What can I do for you today, Molly? Eggs? Cheese? We haven't seen much of you lately."

"I know." She shook her head apologetically. "I break down when I'm in a hurry and buy all the junky supermarket stuff."

"Tsk, tsk," the woman said with a sunny smile. Her skin, clear and wrinkle-free in spite of her age, which was at least fifty by Molly's count, was a testament to her own products. She turned her smile to Alejandro. "You must be the fiancé we're hearing so much about. I'm Katje Micklenburg."

With a courtly gesture, Alejandro bowed slightly over her hand. "I am pleased to make your acquaintance."

Molly said, "It's Jonah I've come to see, actually. We'd like to get married, and my brother is furious, so he's set all the judges against me."

"Ah." She inclined her head. "Now that's a fun kind of visit! Come on up to the house."

As they walked, Alejandro gestured. "Do you mind if I ask questions about your farm?"

"Oh, no! Please, ask away."

"Good."

Molly knew next to nothing about farming or ranching, but the questions he asked all seemed to be intelligent, about various methods of irrigation in the desert, about crops and rainfall, about clay and other soil concerns. Then Katje asked him where he came from, and when he told her, she was off in Spanish, and Alejandro replied cheerfully in the same language. Back and forth, so fast Molly could barely follow a word of it. It made her feel curiously jealous, or maybe only as if she were the outsider here.

But jealousy indicated possessiveness, and Molly needed to be careful about imagining Alejandro belonged to her in any way. A fake marriage for the sake of a green card had nothing in common with the real thing.

As if he sensed her mood, Alejandro looped a casual arm around her shoulders, drawing her into the conversation. "Molly is learning to speak my language," he said. "But she cannot follow so fast, I am certain."

Alejandro's arm felt comfortable around her shoulders. There was none of that awkward bumping of hips that so often occurred when a man and woman tried to loop arms around each other. In the October afternoon, he smelled of the sun-warmed and dusty New Mexico air, a scent as clean as freshly folded laundry. Against her chest, she could feel the vibration of his voice coming out of his rib cage, low and rich, which somehow made her remember the kiss he'd given her in the car in front of her brother's house. A devastating kind of kiss, outrageously sensual. Kissing him, feeling his hand on her face, tasting his tongue in her mouth, she'd been both amazed and appalled at the sudden tightness of her nipples, at the fierce, loud pulse in her groin.

And that reaction was all the more disturbing because the kiss had been staged. No more real than a screen kiss.

No wonder actors fell in love on the set so often.

In love? The words echoed and Molly scowled. No,

she wasn't falling in love. Lust maybe. Too long without a man would do that to a person.

Lust she could survive.

Katje led them up the steps to the cool adobe farm-
house, painted the traditional blue around the windows
and doors to keep out evil spirits. Within, all resem-
blance to a traditional territorial house ended, and it
was plain the farm had indeed begun to pay very, very
well. Saltillo tiles lined the floors, and rare Spanish
colonial weavings alternated with even more rare antique Navajo blankets in gray and red. Alejandro whistled softly. "Only *ricos* live this way in my country,"
he whispered.

"Same in this country," Katje said wryly, then
called, "Jonah!" A rumbling came from somewhere
deep in the house. She sighed. "Make yourselves comfortable. I'll bring him back."

She hurried down the hall and out of sight, leaving
the two of them alone in the living room. Or, Molly
thought with a grin, more likely they called it the "sa-
lon." A lighted painting by an artist out of Taos graced
the wall above the fireplace, and fresh flowers bloomed
on the low tables. The aura of the room was old-style
California.

"This makes me think of Zorro," she commented.

Alejandro did not answer, and she glanced over her
shoulder. He stood by a pair of glass doors that led to
an interior courtyard, and on his face was an unmis-
takable expression of sorrow. "Are you all right?" she
asked.

He turned his head. "This is much like my father's
house," he said. "The house I grew up in." He gestured to the courtyard and Molly joined him to look
out there. A fountain surrounded by banks of vividly

blooming geraniums, pink and red, formed the center of a bricked patio. Long wooden benches reclined in the recessed porch running around it on three sides.

"How beautiful," Molly commented. She stepped through the door to the patio, feeling a cool breeze strike her face.

Alejandro followed her out. "We had a glass table, where we ate breakfast. My mother loved that place. She sat there in the morning to write her letters to all her friends and sisters and cousins, all over Mexico. Then in the evening, she put on an old dress and dug in the flowers, or sometimes just cut them to put in vases." He gave her a sad smile. "I like to think God let her have her patio back when she went to heaven, so she could cut all the flowers she wished."

Molly realized that she had not really believed he was the son of a rich man until he told this story. It shamed her. Again. His bearing was that of a man with education and money behind him. His manners were old-world graceful. He let her go through doors first, like a gentleman, and had even paused by her chair until she sat down, now that he was able. "That's a lovely thought," she said. "I don't think I've imagined what sort of world my husband would like to live in for eternity."

"No?" he asked softly, and turned to look into her face, into her eyes.

Molly caught her breath as he snared her, caught it in wonder at the sheer beauty of those eyes of fire and of peace, set amid those angles that should not work but did. She admired the narrow chin and it seemed as if all chins should be shaped this way, that chins had been defined and perfected in this form.

Time ceased in that strange way of some moments,

and even as she lived it, Molly knew she would re-member it always. The silence of a late October after-noon broken only by the silvery sound of water in the fountain, and the cry of a blue jay overhead. Light made golden by the dust in the air was reflected and deepened by adobe walls, and made his flesh copper, and burnished the crown of his head, revealing the slightest hints of red in his hair.

And she would remember the way he looked at her, looked deep, as if he wanted to know everything that had ever been written on her soul, wanted to explore every hair on her body, wanted to inhale her. It was the purest expression of yearning she had ever seen on anyone's face.

"There you are!"

Katje and Jonah stepped out onto the patio. Alejan-dro's head jerked up, as if he were torn from a dream, and the moment shattered.

But Molly tucked it away in that special box of per-fect moments, and felt as if she'd been given a gift.

Then she realized she ought to have prepared Ale-jandro for the appearance of Jonah. An eccentric, even by valley standards, he was an aging hippie and looked it with his long, gray-and-sand-colored hair, the round wire-framed glasses, the granny shirt made of flowered calico that tied at his neck. He even wore sandals. No one in the outside world would take him seriously, but in the valley, he commanded respect for one simple reason: every bit of success claimed by the farms was his doing. Behind that hippie-grandpa face was the mind of a marketing genius.

He hugged Molly enthusiastically and nearly did the same to Alejandro, but Molly saw the faint but pointed shift of body language as Alejandro straightened stiffly and held out his hand.

"So you're the one stirring up so much talk in town," Jonah said, looking over his glasses. "The wild one who stole Molly's heart."

Tongue in cheek, Alejandro said, "Yeah, that's me, the desperado."

Molly grinned at him. Over Jonah's head, he winked.

"So you folks want to get married, eh? You know when?"

"As soon as possible," Molly said.

"I'm open." Jonah patted his belly, like a Santa Claus of the wedding ceremony. "How's now?"

"You will marry us?" Alejandro said, and Molly heard the surprise.

"Well, I certainly have the power." Jonah winked. "I'm an ordained minister, son. Believe it or not. Divine Science, which my mother said was no real church at all, but I showed her." He chuckled. "What do you say?"

A leap of anticipation and terror made Molly's hands start to tremble suddenly, and she looked at Alejandro with alarm. "What do you think?"

No doubt seeing her sudden worry, he moved close and gave her a slow, very sexy smile. "The sooner the better, no?" He took her hand, and as if he had eyes for no one in the world but Molly Sheffield, a very ordinary-looking nurse from the wilds of New Mexico, he kissed her hand. "Now is good," he said to Jonah.

The old man grinned. "Man, I do so love to see folks in love. Let me grab my tools and I'll be right back. Katje, why don't you have Vivian make us up a snack to celebrate with after?"

Katje, too, was beaming. "That's a great idea. Do you mind?"

Molly smiled. "Not at all."

Alejandro loved standing in the courtyard, with the sun on them, and the sharp scent of geraniums in the air. He liked the shy blush on Molly's face as Katje cut some late roses from a protected bush, red and yellow blossoms that smelled of oranges. He bent to smell them in her hand, and lifted his head with what he hoped was an encouraging smile.

Again he glimpsed her worry, and he understood it. This was a binding. Even if they did not do it for love, the words would be spoken and they would have to look into each other's eyes as they said them. It was a little frightening to imagine.

When Jonah returned, he wore vestments, purple and gold over a long white robe. His feet were still enclosed in rope sandals, like a monk.

To make these kind people believe in their love, Alejandro imagined that his parents were here, that he was confessing love and commitment to a woman who would stand by him, a woman he would not mind growing old with. Thinking of her land, he imagined it was a dowry, while his hands and knowledge and back were the gifts he brought to trade. To make the land live. He took her small white hand in his and closed his other hand over it, and listened carefully as Jonah said the sacred words, words that had been said in almost the same way in so many languages for so many centuries.

He could not say why he did it. But when Jonah prompted him to repeat the phrases of commitment, he said them first in English, then said them again in Spanish. In some odd way, it touched Molly. He saw her eyes take that quicksilver glow, and she gazed at him soberly.

Then—disaster.

"We brought no rings," Alejandro said, aggrieved.

Without missing a beat, Jonah glanced at his wife, and Alejandro saw her nod. Jonah slipped a heavy silver and turquoise ring, set around with stones, from his index finger and gave it to Molly.

When Katje would have taken a ring from the many on her own fingers, Molly stopped her. She took the wedding ring from her right hand and put it in Jonah's palm. "Use this one."

Stricken, Alejandro looked at her fiercely, trying to tell her with his eyes that such a sacrifice was not necessary. She only looked up at him, and gave him a sweet, sure smile.

He gripped her fingers tightly and took the ring from Jonah. He said the words, "With this ring, I thee wed." He lifted the simple gold band to his lips and kissed it, looking into Molly's eyes, then slipped it on her finger.

A single silver tear spilled on her cheek, and when Jonah said, "You may kiss the bride," Alejandro put his hands lightly on her slim shoulders, and pressed his mouth to that tiny creek of sorrow. He tasted salt and imagined that somehow the essence of her was contained in it, and entered him through his mouth.

Then he raised his head. "I am," he said sincerely, "the luckiest man in the world."

The housekeeper managed a lovely spread in less than twenty minutes, and carried it out to the patio, where the light grew deeper and more golden as afternoon reached for evening. Katje poured the wine into glasses, but Alejandro stopped her from pouring it into his. "No, thank you," he said, smiling.

"Not even a little?"

He shook his head, lifting his shoulders apologetically.

"D'you take the oath, man?" Jonah asked. "I got four friends in AA right now."

He gave Molly a bewildered look. "Alcoholics Anonymous," she explained.

"Oh." He smiled. "No, no. I have never liked it…um, the spinning? Even a little makes me uncomfortable."

Molly wondered if he minded that she drank some, and hesitated, thinking she ought to put down the glass. Then she realized she didn't have to change anything about herself for him. He wasn't really her husband.

And if he were?

Sipping the wine, which was excellent, she listened to the light, cheerful conversation around her and thought about that. About changing for someone else. Had she changed for Tim?

"Molly, would you like some of these pears?" Katje asked. "We're experimenting with Bosc varieties."

Molly accepted the offering. Together with the wine, the tastes were like two notes of harmonizing music. "Yes, those are wonderful. Especially with the wine."

From her right, Alejandro suddenly leaned close. "May I taste?"

"Sure." She reached for another slice of pear, but he laughed, the sound low and wicked.

"No, *querida*. Like this," he said, and kissed her.

It was a bold kiss, the hungry kiss of a bridegroom. Molly had to give him credit for superior talent in the timing and acting departments, because she was as non-plussed as a new bride by the richness of that luscious mouth, and before she could think coherently enough to stop herself, had opened her mouth in invitation.

One he took. His tongue swirled in, wicked and probing, then quickly retreated, and he was raising his head, those long-lashed eyes dancing as he tasted her taste on his lips. "Mmm. Very nice."

Molly blushed to the roots of her hair, and looked away, trying desperately to recover her equilibrium. Jonah laughed happily, and Katje slapped his arm. But then she took Molly's hand and one of Alejandro's. "We see many couples. But not very many have that light about them the way you two do." She tightened her fingers. "May God bless your union with all things," she said poetically. "And let yours be an example of those who wish to love all their lives."

Molly looked at Alejandro, feeling guilt at the seriousness of the blessing. This was not what they had planned, not at all. In his eyes, she saw the same disturbance, and he gave her a subtle nod.

Soon, they would take their leave and end this mockery.

Chapter 9

They were subdued on the way back to Molly's house, and without speaking, moved to different parts of the house to give each other time to absorb this new status between them.

From the phone in the bedroom, Molly called Lynette, needing to touch base with some kind of normality. "Hey, girl," she said lightly when Lynette answered.

"Molly! I'm so glad you called right now. I can talk for a little since Josh went to the grocery store for me."

Molly's heart plummeted. "I guess that means he's still very angry with me."

"Oh, don't worry, honey. You know how he is. He sees the world in black and white." She giggled. "You fell to the dark side."

Molly chuckled.

"Oh, that sounded bad, didn't it?" Lynette fussed.

"I didn't mean it that way, like dark person. I meant like Darth Vader."

"I knew what you meant." She frowned. "You don't have to be politically correct with me, Lynette."

"I know. Or I mean, I think I do." She sighed. "Never mind. Josh is mad right now, but he'll miss you and decide maybe he can overlook your sins."

Sins. Molly wondered if that was Lynette's feeling, too. "Well, he'll have to, because we got married today."

"You did? How—"

"How did I do it when Josh managed to turn all the judges against it? I went to Jonah Micklenburg." The thought of the ceremony, so warm and colorful for all that it had been staged, warmed the hollow places in her. "It was beautiful. I wish you could have been there."

"Moll, are you sure about this? He's very cute, and I liked how nice he was with my kids, but really— what can he offer you?"

"He makes me laugh, Lynette, and he knows all kinds of things I don't know. He can teach me to speak Spanish, and maybe I'll plant my fields, finally. It was what Tim wanted."

"Well, I hope you aren't setting yourself up for heartbreak. I hate to think he's just using you to get a green card."

Molly's temper snapped. "Honestly, Lynette, you act like I'm fifteen, thinking about sleeping with the local bad boy." She shook her head. "Alejandro's not like that. He has...honor."

"Mmm." The word was skeptical.

Stung, Molly simply said, "You'll see."

"I hope so, Molly. I want you to be happy." Urgently she said, "Josh is home. I gotta go."

Molly hung up, frowning. *I want you to be happy,* Lynette said. But if that were true, wouldn't she be rejoicing? Wouldn't she have stood up for Molly instead of repeating all Josh's words?

Vaguely disturbed, she moved to the bureau and began taking out the things that had belonged to Tim. Some of them would fit Alejandro, and she stacked them in a chair for him to try on, leaving the drawers empty for him to store things as he wished. It was a necessary step—she didn't think for one minute that they'd escape without an official inquiry, and it was best to be ready. His things should be in her bedroom.

But the work was for her hands, so her mind could mull over the disturbing new thoughts that had surfaced today. She thought about her brother, so intent on making her do what he considered in her best interest that he'd get her in trouble rather than let her choose her own way.

She scowled, the stirrings making her very uncomfortable. She'd lived in this town her entire life, and her parents had been here for ten years before that. Except for the brief time she'd spent at nursing school, she'd lived right here for almost thirty years. In Vallejos, she was safe, secure. She knew everyone and they all knew her.

And until now, she'd lived an exemplary life by town standards. Even in her grief, when she'd wanted to scream and cry and become so hysterical someone had to carry her away, she'd behaved with calm dignity, burying her pain where none could see it or be upset by it.

Her heart beat a little too fast. Didn't she want their

good opinion? Didn't she want to belong to her community?

Of course. But something else had surfaced when she found Alejandro, bleeding and distraught, on her land that day. She had acted from no prompting but her own. How many times in her life had that really happened? How often had she listened only to herself?

She sank onto the bed. While she loved nursing, she had been nudged into it by her mother's friends, who had wanted Molly to follow in her mother's footsteps. She'd mounted a token protest about art school, but the point was made that Molly, alone in the world, needed to be practical.

Which was true. Where would she be now if she'd studied art in Colorado instead of nursing in Albuquerque?

And then there was Tim. He had been her high-school beau. They had met in eighth grade and started going together the following year. She'd loved him, but in college, had hoped to date others. The request had wounded him so much that she'd backed off. And wasn't she glad now? She had not wasted their very short time together.

The traitorous thoughts, let free for the first time, suddenly spilled out in a rush, and she thought of a hundred tiny choices she'd wanted to make for herself, but had allowed someone else to talk her out of.

Usually Tim.

Holding one of his shirts in her hands, she remembered the three-story Victorian house in town that she'd hoped to buy instead of this land. The house of her heart.

It stood a few blocks from the house in town where she'd grown up. For years, Molly had walked past it on her way to school or the market; she'd spun stories of it; she'd drawn it many times, in many weathers. Locals said it was haunted by the ghost of a wronged woman. When it had come on the market just before she and Tim got married, she'd gone to him full of excitement, knowing he had the skills to put the house to rights, that they could have a huge brood of children to fill it.

He'd agreed to go look at the place, but while Molly ran from room to room, imagining wallpaper and the pleasure of refinishing the old cherry-wood paneling, he'd muttered and scowled all the way through. He didn't hate it, he said. He just didn't love it. And then he took her to this house, to this land.

To her credit, she'd not given up easily on that one. She'd wanted that house with her whole heart—no, more than that, she felt as though it belonged to her, that it was meant to be her house. She'd argued that Tim could still have his farm and land—for the same price of this hundred acres and the house, they could have had the Victorian and an equally rich, but slightly smaller, plot of land just outside of town.

But she lost. And three years later, when the house had been condemned for the wiring, Molly had wept bitterly.

It still stood, barely. Neglected and haunted and lonely, waiting for her. She still drew it sometimes. When Tim died, leaving a large insurance settlement, she'd almost taken a portion of the money to the real estate broker and asked to buy it. But that time, Lynette had talked her out of it—pointing out that Molly had enough on her plate without adding a white elephant like an abandoned Victorian.

And now the pattern was repeating itself. She'd

made a choice to help a man in need, and she'd done it from her heart, because it felt like the right thing to do. By acting, she'd also saved a little girl, who might have died out there in those fields waiting for her deported uncle to come back to her. She'd taken a drastic step this afternoon, it was true. Maybe some would even say it was wrong.

But Molly, for once in her life, was acting on her gut instincts, and this time, by damn, she wasn't going to let the pressure of the group make her back down.

This time, she would fight to the very end for what she believed.

After a couple of hours spent reading, Molly came into the kitchen, where Alejandro sat, sketching something on a big tablet of paper. He was left-handed, which she had not noticed till now.

He looked up, pushing hair from his face. "Ah. There you are. Feeling better?"

Molly nodded. "You?"

"Yes. This makes me feel better, always. Come see."

"What is it?" Molly stood to one side, looking over his shoulder. "It looks like a map."

"In a way." He turned it for her, and the view made sense. "It is an idea of things to do for your land, so it will give back to you, very easily, with hardly any work from you."

Unsettled, Molly sank into a chair at the head of the table and accepted the sketch. "I'm not sure I really want to do anything, really. I like the land the way it is."

He dismissed that with one hand. "You want to keep some sage and cactus, you could have some. No problem." Clearly caught in his own vision, he gave her another sketch, this one illustrating a fenced area with a chicken coop. A rooster sat on a fence post.

"You're very good," she said in surprise. The lines were strong, clear, clean, drawn with a kind of power that seemed to always elude Molly. In comparison, her paintings were very timid indeed. "Have you done this work professionally?"

"A long time ago they taught me art."

"In school?"

"Yeah. I did not finish." He shuffled through the stack—he must have been sketching since they'd returned—and pulled out another. "Bees."

A tight sensation drew up her back. "Alejandro, stop."

He looked at her, wariness replacing enthusiasm. "I did something wrong, no?"

"Not wrong. I just…don't know if I'm ready for all this. So much change."

"Ah." With calm dignity, he gathered the drawings. "I am sorry. I did not think." With a smile, he said, "My mind…sometimes I think I know what is right for everything, and do not listen."

"I appreciate the gesture."

He nodded, and Molly saw that now it was he who was moving a little stiffly. "I've offended you," she said.

"No." As if to emphasize that, he also shook his head. "No. I only wish to do something to give back to you what you have given me. I am a man, and too proud." He shrugged. "I will think of something."

"You don't have to hurry, Alejandro. We're stuck with this for a year at least."

"*Sí.* You are right. Plenty of time." He lifted his

chin, and she found herself noticing the impossible broadness of his shoulders beneath the shirt she had chosen for him. "But, Josefina and me, we are not stuck. We are rescued."

"I didn't mean it like that."

"I know." He stood and picked up the materials. "Another day, huh?"

"Sure." She nodded. "I remember why I came in here. You need to move your things into my room. In case."

"Ah. I'm glad you thought of that." He nodded. "Do you wish for me to do it now?"

"Yes. I think I'm going to go to bed."

"It has been a long day."

The conversation was beginning to sound like an entry-level language practice. *"Sí, señor,"* she said impulsively. *"Yo soy muy...tiredo."*

The rigidness in his posture eased the slightest bit and he smiled. *"Cansado."*

She repeated it and stood. "Let me show you where to put your things. You can settle everything while I take a shower."

As they walked up the hallway, Alejandro, limping rather pronouncedly tonight, said, "Not even chickens, Molly? They are very cheap."

"What would I do with them? I don't know how to even kill a chicken."

"Oh, you would not kill one for a long time. Not till she was old and gave no more eggs. Someone could do it for you." He halted to let her go into the room first. "Josefina is very good. It was her job once. She can pluck them, too. So fast."

"Josefina can kill and pluck a chicken?" Molly made a face. "And she's eight. Boy, do I feel dumb."

"No!" he laughed. "She is a working child. I have not liked that she had to work so much, but it was what we had to do. The chickens, she would like feeding them better. Getting the eggs." He warmed again. "The eggs are why the chickens, Saint Molly. Fresh eggs. Your own."

She laughed. "You don't get it. I have land, and this house but I don't know anything. I don't even know if I would like having chickens!"

He held up his hands, smiling. "Okay. No more. I won't bother you anymore. Here?" He pointed to the bureau and closet, and then halted, looking around himself. "This is beautiful!" He glanced at Molly. "Your husband again?"

She nodded, crossing her arms against the feeling of intimacy brought on by his presence in this room. He seemed so much larger here. "He made everything in here—paneled the walls, made the bureau and bed to match."

Alejandro lifted a hand to stroke one of the four posts on the bed, his fingers caressing the velvety grain—a rare birch. He leaned close to examine it, then whistled softly. "A man who did work this beautiful— I think his heaven would be filled with wood and tools, to make a throne for God."

The words pierced her utterly, and she made a soft sound. "You must go," she said suddenly, recognizing that her emotions were highly incendiary and could blow at any second.

He raised his head and she saw the bewilderment in his eyes. "I seem to step wrong every time," he said sadly. "I am very sorry for that, Saint Molly." He moved to the door. "Good night." He paused. "I would like to call Josefina and tell her good-night. May

I do that?'' Raising his hand, the one with the turquoise ring on it, he touched her face. ''Thank you for everything, Molly. You are a good woman. If you think of anything I can do, you must tell me, no?''

''I will,'' she said. ''I promise.'' She could see it sat ill with him to be so dependent on her, and made a mental note to see if there was work available for him right away. It would ease his pride to bring in money. Then she smiled. ''Actually, there are two things you can do. I draw, but not like you. I want to know how to put authority into my work. Can you show me?''

''Yes!'' Light shone in his face. ''I would like that.''

''And the other—I really would like to learn to speak Spanish. That's something I know you can teach me.''

''No problem.'' He winked. ''We will start tomorrow on those things. Now you go, take your shower, and I will settle my things, and you will not even know I am here tonight.'' He touched her hair briefly, and stepped away.

It was exactly what she wanted, Molly thought. And not only had he seen her wish, but had not been offended by it. An unusual man.

Alejandro slept deeply and well, and to his surprise, the sun was full in the sky when he awakened. Smelling coffee, he put sweats on over his boxers and limped to the kitchen. The coffee machine—he would have to ask how it worked—was steaming and he poured a cup.

Through the window over the sink, he glimpsed Molly at work in her garden. Her hair was tied back in its usual braid. He'd only seen it down that one time. The morning was very warm, and there was sweat staining the back of her T-shirt. Smiling, he limped to the door and wandered out to the porch. ''There is a good sight," he called out. "A woman hard at work, so early in the morning."

She laughed. "Good morning, lazybones."

"Lazy?" he repeated mockingly. "Me?"

Brushing a tendril of hair from her eyes, she straightened. "I've already weeded the whole garden, eaten breakfast and washed a load of clothes, *señor*."

He liked her in this teasing mood. Her face was flushed with exercise, and the casual, loose-fitting clothes outlined her body very nicely. "But I have been wounded, *señora*. A man must heal."

"You look like you feel a hundred times better this morning," she said, eyeing him with her nurse's face. "You must have slept well."

"Like a baby. And I told you, I am strong." But he did not think it was the sleep that made him feel this way. It was hope, a chance to make things better for him and Josefina. He mugged a bodybuilder's pose. "Sexy, too, no?"

Her eyes skittered over the expanse of his chest and just as quickly skittered away. He grinned, rubbing his flat belly. "A little overwhelming, though. I understand."

She laughed. "Vanity, thy name is man." She slapped her gloves together, and the motion made her breasts, loosely clasped in some thin undergarment, move a little. He yanked his gaze away, wondering why those small, cup-shaped breasts held so much fascination.

"I've been thinking about your chickens," she said.

"Yes?"

"If you want to build a henhouse and try it, I guess I might like having a rooster alarm clock."

He laughed happily. "That's good! Yes, you will

like it. We can find out today who has them for sale.''
He sipped his coffee. "We will go see Josefina, no?"

"Of course."

"And will you go to work?"

"No. Cathy gave me two weeks off to take care of all this."

"Good. I would like to work, I think. I am tired of sitting and sitting. You have things I can fix here, no? That dripping sink, maybe?"

She smiled. "Sure. I'll put you to work. Get everything shipshape before you go off to real life."

Real life. It seemed, suddenly, as he admired her in her garden, with sun falling down on her many-colored head, a very bleak prospect.

Chapter 10

They spent most of the day with Josefina, who was, in the way of sick children the world over, cranky and irritable at the confinement. She insisted she felt fine, that she just wanted to go home and see her dog.

At noon, Molly ducked out to go to the local five-and-dime. She bought a basket and filled it with all kinds of little-girl things—coloring books and paper dolls, crayons and markers, a pretty doll with some extra outfits. Remembering Alejandro's comment about Josefina's intelligence, she also picked out some easy readers and a math workbook.

On the way out, she stopped by the stuffed animals to pick out a dog. It was surprising how many there were. Remembering Wiley's comments about a little mutt, she found a small brown-and-white one with a felt tongue hanging out of its smiling mouth.

At the checkout, she grinned at the checker, a woman in her sixties whose children Molly had baby-sat during her teens. "Hi, Mrs. Nolan. How're the boys?"

The blue eyes were cold behind her glasses. "They're just fine, thank you."

Molly's immediate impulse was to try to make things right—explain her actions, paste on her brightest fake smile and remind the woman that she was still Molly Sheffield, everybody's favorite girl next door.

She resisted. "I'm glad," she said as if she had not noticed the hostility. "Please tell them I said hello."

There was no reply. Feeling vaguely triumphant over her ability to remain strong in the face of community disapproval, Molly paid and drove back to the hospital.

At the desk, she stopped to talk to the floor nurse. "How's she doing, Annie?"

Annie, a Latina in her twenties, fresh from nursing school, shook her head. "It's TB for sure. The tests came back." She sighed heavily. "The worry now is infection. She has an elevated white-cell count, and the doctor is concerned about pneumonia."

"I see. Did you tell her uncle?"

"Yeah. He seemed very worried about it. Maybe you can reassure him that we should be able to treat it with no trouble." Annie glanced over her shoulder and leaned close. "Where did you find him? He's absolutely gorgeous! I want one."

Molly laughed and wiggled her eyebrows. "He doesn't have a brother, but maybe a cousin, huh?"

Annie sighed. "And he's so polite. I never meet polite men."

"I'd better get in there if he's worrying." Molly hauled the basket off the counter and went down to the room. When she pushed open the door, her gaze fell first on Alejandro, standing at the bedside, reading a ragged copy of a picture book to Josefina. He halted at a word, and shook his head. "This one, I don't know, *hija.* You have to help me."

Josefina laughed. "It's *white,* Tío. You know that."

"Oh, *white!* Sure, sure, I see now." He looked up and caught Molly's eye. "Lucky for me I have such a smart child to help me, huh?" His tone was light, but Molly saw the lines of strain around his mouth. And a moment later, when Josefina coughed, the sound deep and obviously painful, Molly understood why.

Still, no good would come of him wearing himself out entirely. His own health was fragile. "Did your uncle eat, like I told him to?" Molly asked Josefina.

"No." Molly saw with concern that there was a faint sheen on her forehead. "I told him to, but he wouldn't."

"I ate your pudding!"

"Big deal, right, kiddo?" Molly put the basket on the side of the bed and took out a bag of hamburgers. "I'm pretty smart, too." She gave Alejandro the bag and a cola, and started taking out the other things for Josefina, who was quite happy with all of it, especially the little dog, but tired so quickly that Molly was genuinely alarmed. "You want to just watch some TV for a little while, kiddo?"

Josefina nodded. Molly clicked on the set, found some cartoons and tucked blankets around the girl more carefully. She inclined her head toward the door, looking at Alejandro, and he stood. "We'll be back in a few minutes, little one, okay?"

The child, hand tucked under her chin, nodded dully.

In the hall, he said, "Tell me."

Molly knew better than to mince words with him. "It looks like pneumonia. We have to let her rest. If you don't want to leave the hospital entirely, I can understand that, but you have to take care of yourself, too. You can't let yourself get too tired.''

''I am well now.''

''No,'' she said firmly. ''You really are not. And if you'd like to be back in bed, flat on your back, keep skipping meals and worrying.''

A faint grin turned up one side of his mouth, and he touched her upper arm with one finger. ''Bossy.''

''You'd better believe it.''

But unfortunately, Josefina's condition worsened dramatically over the next couple of hours. By supper, she was moved to ICU, with oxygen, and permitted a visitor only once an hour for ten minutes.

Alejandro stood there for the whole ten minutes each hour. Most of that time, she was sleeping and he could only hold her hand, murmuring prayers, over and over. Reckless prayers, offered in desperation to all the saints he could remember. He listened to the swoosh and beeps of the machines with a sense of breathlessness, as if it were his own chest infected. He wished it was. He took the medal off his neck and put it around her wrist, and prayed some more.

In between, he dozed in the waiting room, and Molly stayed with him, holding his hand sometimes, attempting to reassure him. She left for a while and came back with food, which he ate mechanically. He wanted to send her away, wished he did not need her again, so soon, that one day, somehow, he would be the strong one. She would think him a weak man indeed, and he was not.

Finally, a little past midnight, the fever broke and Josefina seemed out of danger for a little while. The doctor, reporting the news in a face that seemed sincere, told Alejandro this would be a good time to go home and get some sleep. "Maybe by the time you come back in the morning, she'll be able to eat with you."

"You will tell her I am coming back? And if she—"

"I'll call you." The doctor looked at Molly with a smile Alejandro found vaguely insulting, and he scowled, tugging his arm away from Molly's hand. They were treating him as if he were the child.

"Does my worry amuse you?" he asked pointedly.

"On the contrary, Mr. Sosa, I find it refreshing." The doctor pursed her lips. "However, it would not take a trained professional to see that you are dead on your feet and need to get some rest. Those are my orders. Let your wife take you home."

His wife. He had almost forgotten. Wiping a hand over his face, he nodded. "I am sorry."

On the way to the house, Alejandro saw that Molly, too, was exhausted. Blue shadows lay under her eyes. Impulsively, he reached across the seat. "Thank you for staying with me. It was good not to be alone."

She attempted a smile that fell short of her eyes.

Inside, Molly threw her keys on the table and kicked off her shoes, then moved to the kitchen. Alejandro followed more slowly, his body reminding him forcefully that he was not yet healed, and there was, too, a hollowness in his chest that he couldn't quite pinpoint until he also drank a glass of water and they were standing side by side, dull-witted and staring sightlessly at the gray shapes of moon-washed lavender beds outside the window.

Suddenly, the full force of it all hit Alejandro, and with a strangled sound, he reached for the counter. "If she had been outside another day," he said roughly, "she would have died."

"Yes," Molly whispered.

Something in her posture, coupled with his own need for human touch, made him reach for her, pull her next to him. And there was not even a hint of resistance. She flowed into his embrace, and put her head on his shoulder with a sigh.

It eased the hollowness in him, and he closed his eyes, inexpressibly weary, drawing comfort from the warmth and softness of her. In an ancient motion of comfort, they rocked ever so slightly.

"I can tell you now that it's over," she said quietly, "and she's out of danger." She paused. "But she almost died tonight. I have never prayed so hard in all my life."

It pierced him, and he rubbed his cheek against her hair. "So did I."

And there was no more need for words. They simply leaned together, finding support and comfort from the other. Vaguely, he wondered why humans needed this, needed to feel the breath of another, feel the warmth of blood below flesh, the assurance of life continuing.

The need for sleep edged into his brain, sucked will from his muscles. He raised his head. "Molly, will you let me sleep beside you? Only sleep, I promise." He touched her hair. "I want to hold you."

She simply nodded, took his hand and led him to her bedroom. He took off his shirt, and would have left on his jeans, but she gave him a half smile. "I've already seen everything."

But more modest than he, she took a flannel night-shirt into the bathroom and came back, suddenly shy, he could tell. Carefully, he did not look at her bare legs, and held out a hand. "Only sleep, Saint Molly. We both need to touch."

Without another word of protest, she slid under the covers and across the bed into his arms. Her head fit neatly into his shoulder, and her small hand rested against his chest, and with a sigh, he let sleep come on him.

When Molly awakened, the first thing she became aware of was Alejandro's breath against her neck. There was not a single second of confusion over exactly who it was in the bed with her, the bed she'd only shared with one man her whole life.

And there was no mistaking the feel of his long-fingered hand resting loosely upon her hip. No mistake in the rush of feelings that overtook her when she realized she was lying here with the man who, if she were honest, had occupied center stage of her fantasies for several days now. Against her bare calf, she felt the silky hair of his shin. His soft breath, warm and moist on her neck, made her imagine how close his mouth was to her flesh.

She ached to turn, simply roll over in the nest of blankets, and put her hands on him. Instead, savoring the moment as it was, she simply lay very still and gloried in the surprise that was Alejandro Sosa. Every facet of him surprised her, but especially this. How many men would have slept beside a woman without trying something? How many men would have been so respectful of her needs and wishes in every little thing?

What an odd freedom he'd given her!

His hand moved on her hip, moved away, and Molly felt him getting up. Bereft, she turned. "I didn't know you were awake."

With his back to her, that long, butter-smooth, golden back, he said, "I have been awake for a long time, Saint Molly. I am going to take a shower and make coffee for you." Still keeping his back to her, he slipped into his jeans, then turned and tugged the cover back over her shoulder. "Sleep a little longer."

She gazed up at him sleepily, hungrily, wishing for the courage to pull the covers back and invite him to crawl back into bed with her. For a moment, as he stood there, looking down, she thought he was going to do it, even without her invitation. Then he smiled. "Sleep some more," he said, and left her.

When he was safely gone, she pulled a pillow over her head and groaned. If nerves were visible, she would look like a porcupine. Every single one stood on alert, distended, ready. She needed his hands on her. His mouth. His body. It was the only thing that would soothe those nerves back into place.

She pushed the pillow down harder on her face. The smell of him lingered in it, sending the longing up one more notch, making her remember the way his long, copper limbs had looked when she bathed him, when his black hair was drawn back from that elegantly arranged face.

The water came on in the bathroom. Right by her head. On the other side of that wall he was naked, all six feet two inches of muscled flesh. Right now, water was spilling over him, *all* over him. His neck. His beautiful shoulders. His mouth. His sex.

Her skin was on fire. What was wrong with her? In disgust, she got up, threw on her robe and started unweaving her tangled braid. She was crazy. He was kind and honorable and virtuous. She was a sex-crazed female who couldn't think how to seduce him.

Maybe, she thought, yanking a brush through her hair, he wasn't all that interested. He'd certainly had plenty of opportunity—and it wasn't like men of any culture were slow to pick up on those signals. She'd been blipping red-hot since the first night she'd lusted over him in the back room, when he had ostensibly been just a patient she was nursing back to health.

Get over it, she told herself with a glare, and flung open the door, stomping down the hallway in her bare feet, studiously ignoring the sound of the shower behind the bathroom door.

Coffee. She needed coffee, fast. And a good walk, maybe. She scowled, running her tongue over her teeth. And her toothbrush. Ugh.

She started the coffee and leaned against the counter, glaring at the machine while she waited for Alejandro to emerge. When he did, with his hair wet-combed straight back, and his jaw shaved and his blastedly gorgeous chest bare and damp, she brushed by him abruptly and went into the bathroom. She scrubbed her teeth with the same violence she'd used on her hair, washed her face until it stung—

And she could still feel the brush of his breath on her neck. Could feel the ghostly image of his shin against the back of her leg. Felt the imprint of his hand on her hip.

I have been awake a long time.

"You idiot," she said into the mirror. He was honorable in such an old-world way that a jaded American like Molly had a hard time even recognizing the depth of it when it was right under her nose. She thought of him carefully keeping his body turned away from her, thought of his rush to the shower.

A cold shower?

With a slight sense of giddiness, she took off her robe and her gown. She washed her breasts and arms and private places, then dusted a musky talcum powder over her body. Then, naked below her loosely tied robe, she went to find him.

He leaned on the kitchen sink, an unusual brooding expression on his face, one he quickly hid when she came into the room. "Ah," he said, smiling. "There you are. Do you wish my good coffee, or this machine kind?"

Molly swallowed. It had been one thing to imagine, in the privacy of the bathroom, seducing him. It was quite another to actually do it.

To her despair, she found she didn't have the courage.

Brightly she said, "Well, the machine kind is already made." She opened a cupboard, embarrassingly aware of her nakedness below the robe, and took out two mugs.

He was quiet as she poured first his, then her own. Her skin flushed under his gaze, and she wanted, more than breathing, for him to kiss her. Touch her.

He brushed his hand over her hair, down her back. "You never wear it like this," he said. "Why?"

Molly stirred sugar in her coffee. "Too much trouble." She lifted her head to smile, stupidly and brightly, once again, and halted.

Alejandro, bare to the waist, held his coffee in one hand. In his other, he grasped a fistful of her hair. His eyes were far beyond liquid as he stared down at her— they were lava. Molten. For a moment, he only looked at her, then in a gesture both considered and primal, he lifted the small fistful of hair to his face and rubbed it across his mouth.

Her hips went suddenly fluid.

"I am trying, Molly, to be strong." He swallowed and put the cup down on the counter, then took hers and put it down, too. With one hand, he drew a line from her throat down to the opening of her robe, which was lower than she had believed, low enough to reveal the obviously naked swell of a breast at the opening. "I do not think you wish me to be strong any longer."

"No," she whispered.

His eyes closed for one moment, then he let go of a breath, as if he'd held it a long time, and bent down to touch his lips to hers. They kissed, lips to lips, that gentleness of greeting, and then he pressed closer, a heaviness to his breath, and backed her into the counter. The kiss ignited, pushing from one second to the next far beyond civility or gentleness or greeting into a roaring expression of passion, for her and for him. Their teeth clicked at the urgent connection, and Molly lifted her hands to his licorice-black hair, taking it in her fists, pulling him closer.

He hauled her against him, as if by pressing close they would meld, and she cried out, wishing for more. He broke the kiss and lifted his head, the dark eyes grave.

Molly thought of his face that first day, the way it had struck her, like an arrow through the heart, and even then, she had known this time would come. She put a hand on his cheek, wordless as she stroked the high arch of bone below his eye, let her thumb drift to touch his chin, cleanly shaven.

He held her gaze as he moved backward, then covered her throat with his hand, his touch light as he slid his palm downward, flat between her breasts, then lower still, using his wrist, then his other hand, to untie the robe. It hung open but covering her breasts, for a long, long moment. "I ached, all night, to touch you," he said. "To see you."

"So did I," she whispered. He pushed away the fabric covering her breasts. For one agonizing moment, she worried that her breasts would be too small, too ordinary, too pale, but then he made a low, pleased sound, and those long-fingered elegant hands lifted, cupped the soft weight.

"Touch me," he said, and bent to take her mouth in a deep, bruising kind of kiss, a violence of need she welcomed with a violence of her own. She opened her hands on his body, and met his kiss even as her greedy palms explored the whole of his back, the muscles and spine, and touched his waist, and lightly skimmed over his bruised ribs. With a low groan, he shoved the robe from her shoulders and pulled her next to him, chest to chest, arms entangled, brushing, exploring, even as he kissed her and kissed her and kissed her. His member thrust aggressively against her belly, and she rubbed against it, lost in the glory of the fury the contact brought out, the need.

As if both acted with one mind, they broke apart and joined hands and moved to the bed in the back room, flooded with sunlight that poured from the eastern sky in buckets, bucketsful of liquid, gold light. Alejandro stopped her when she would have lain on the bed. "Wait," he said urgently. She saw him swallow, and his eyes burned as he skimmed her panties from her body, then pulled her hair around her shoulders, over her breasts. "I thought of this so often," he whispered, touching her nipples through her hair. "So many colors. Sunlight and clay and roses." He cupped her breasts in their cloak of hair, lifting them, in no rush.

Her breath came in quick, shallow pants, and her legs were made of tissue, but it was devastatingly erotic to stand naked and pagan in the sunlight while a man who was still mostly dressed touched her as if he had never dreamed of anything so beautiful. And again she knew, even as the moment burned through her that she would never forget—never—the way Alejandro made her feel right now.

She lowered her lids against the brilliance of light melting over her, and gasped softly as he bent his head and suckled her breast through her hair, lingeringly, as if there was nothing he would ever have to do but this. He suckled her neck, and kissed a line between her breasts, knelt and lingered over her belly, putting the side of his face against it for a moment, his hand on her hips. He kissed her thighs, pulled back and looked at her sex, brushed his fingers over the hair.

It made her dizzy. She steadied herself by grasping his shoulders, and the reflected red of sunlight beneath her eyelids burned all else away as he grasped her hips and kissed between her legs. She cried out, pleased, but doubly hungry, and her body began to shiver. With arms made fierce by need, she pulled him up and they fell together on the bed.

"Take off your pants," she said, and grabbed them by their hems. He laughed when his hands were not quick enough, and Molly helped him, hauling clothes from him with a boldness that was not like her.

Or maybe it was. Maybe this was truly the Molly that lived inside the shell all these years, a Molly who could stand naked, draped only in sunlight and hair as she gazed down at her lover.

She made a sound of pain at the revelation of him, all of him lying on that bed as she remembered. She used her fingers to touch what her eyes admired—the shelf of collarbone and triangular swath of hair across his chest. She brushed the bruises, purple and yellow, on his side, and the smooth, flat, copper belly and the dark weight of his aroused sex growing out of its silky nest.

''I've never seen a man who was so beautiful,'' she whispered, and with a sense of reverence, she knelt over him and kissed his throat, and his chest, and his chin, expressing with her hands what she could not say—that never had God made a man more perfect than he. Never.

He touched her hair, pulled her to his mouth, breathing softly, *''Dios,''* before he kissed her, the power in his arms fierce and unyielding as he guided her to mount him. It made her briefly shy, and she protested, but he touched her waist, her lips, and she remembered that his leg would be too weak for a more traditional sort of joining. She closed her eyes against her shyness, at the sense of being utterly exposed as she let him guide himself into her.

The shock of pleasure was so deep, so intense that she cried out, even as he groaned, low and rich in his throat, and Molly's shyness disappeared as she threw her head back, and felt him, responded to his subtle movements, began to move.

As if he could not bear to be so far apart, he reached for her, pulling her down into his kiss, and somehow, somehow, they found the exquisite rhythm, breaking and falling and tumbling together, dust motes on a river of sunlight, hair and mouths and deep cries. Molly found tears washing from her eyes and did not halt them, for they were tears of joy and freedom. And love.

Oh, love. Spent, they folded together, and Molly let

the tears wash from her eyes down her cheeks to his chest, felt the gentleness of his big strong capable hands, and knew beyond the faintest doubt that she had only been waiting, all of her days, for this man to come into her life and set her free. In a rush of gratitude, she lifted her wet face and put her hands on his face and stared down at him for a long moment.

"Gracias," she said softly, and kissed his wide, generous mouth, watched his eyes with their long black lashes close as if in pain. *"Gracias,"* she whispered again.

Wordless, he kissed her fiercely, pulled her tight against him, breathed into her hair.

Chapter 11

For a long time, Alejandro simply held his saint close against his body, unwilling to release the spirit he had momentarily captured. He wrapped his long arms around her naked shoulders and breathed in the smell of her hair, scattered over his chest and chin.

He had wished to make love to her all night long—no, before that. Since the first time they kissed—but he had not known it would shatter him so. He had expected bashfulness, slowness, an exploration of tiny moves to bigger ones, a long slow night of learning.

Instead, it seemed he had always known her, as if they were old lovers, come together again after a long, long time of waiting. He had known exactly where to touch her, how, when, and it seemed she had known. how to return his gestures. Only the smallest of moves and they realigned in new harmony.

A vision of her, head thrown back as she mounted him, burned through his veins and stirred in his newly spent organ, and in response, he pulled her up close to kiss her, and touch her, his need flaming all over again. He lifted on one elbow over her and touched the tracks of tears on her face, wondering if she wept over remembering her husband or in release, that release she had thanked him so earnestly for. Her thanks made him feel hollow for a moment, and that hollowness came back as he looked at her, filled with a pained sort of wonder at her beauty, at the dazzling, blinding sense of love he felt toward her.

He loved too soon, too fast, too deep, and kissing her had been too much. But he had learned well to hide his true feelings, and he did it now, with a quick, wicked grin that spoke in a language that was less dangerous—desire. Women loved to be desired fiercely, and he could give her that, give her that which she most needed. "My blood is still boiling," he said, and kissed her, hoping she tasted lust instead of the worship he could not help offering.

But he could not help moving in that sacred place, adoring her taste and her breath, her soft skin and surprisingly vigorous cries, loving the sweetness of her need, the fury of her climax, could not help kneeling at the altar of his Saint Molly, who had not saved him at all, but made him fall to a purgatory where he could not speak his heart.

Josefina stirred from a light sleep to find her uncle back again at the side of her bed. He did not see her wake up, and so she could watch him for a minute, trying to decide why he seemed so different tonight. He wore a red shirt that was new and very nice with his black hair, which was clean and shiny even in the low light. He was very handsome, she thought, and not just because he was her uncle. She was not as deaf as grown-ups always thought, and she heard the women talk about him. Sometimes they said things she did not strictly understand, but she knew what they meant.

But now, he was even more than handsome. He made her think of something just out of reach. He had his guitar in his hands and was tuning it softly, and he looked happy in a way she couldn't remember ever seeing. Not a big-grin kind of happy, but as if he was listening to something beautiful inside him.

Josefina thought of kind Molly, who had brought her dolls and books, and had strong hands, like a mother. She hoped it was Molly that made her uncle look this way.

"Will you play me a song, Tío?" she said, yawning.

He jumped up, his face blazing now, and came over to take her hand, which he put to his mouth and kissed. "*Hija!* Do you feel better?"

Josefina considered. Coughed once, to check. "It doesn't hurt so much now."

"Good. It is almost time for your dinner. I will play you something while you eat, eh?" He gave her that look that made her know, deep, deep down where no one could take it from her, that she was the most wonderful little girl in the whole wide world. "I worried, *hija*. So much."

"I'm okay now."

"So I see. Hey, your little dog is getting spoiled by the farmer! He took him to the doctor and got shots for him and everything. Did you give her a name?"

Josefina shook her head. "I couldn't think too good. Does she miss me?"

"Yes. She came to me and said, 'Where is my Josefina, my little girl? I need her to love me and pet me and take care of me.'" He used a little-dog kind of voice, and Josefina laughed, which made her cough. Kinda hard for a minute.

"I need to play you a sad song, I think," he said, and gave her a mock smile. "No more laughing until you get better."

"No," she protested. "Play flamenco!"

He grinned and winked at her. "Only if you promise not to dance."

She laughed, which started her coughing again. "Okay."

Molly sat with Annie, allowing Alejandro and Josefina some time alone together. It was quiet in the ward, and they played a round of War with a battered deck of cards.

The music drifted down the hall like a siren song, exotic and seductive, making both nurses lift their heads and turn toward it. For a moment, they simply looked toward the sound, as if expecting the notes to somehow become visible. Then, as if inhabiting a single body, they dropped their cards and moved toward it.

Molly felt the excitement of the music in her chest and along the nerves on the back of her neck and a strange, hot prick of tears in her eyes.

At the open door of Josefina's room, both Annie and Molly paused, giving a moment's holy silence to the picture he presented, his hair so black against the red of his shirt, his lean body so right with the guitar cradled into it, his fingers flying. And that face, that face that had proved her downfall, was alight with zest and pure happiness in a way she had not yet seen.

Annie whispered, "I am *so* jealous."

He caught sight of them and turned himself toward them a little, grinning as he finished with a flourish. Josefina clapped. "More!"

"Is that flamenco?" Annie said. "I heard it in Spain."

He bowed. *"Sí, señorita."* His gaze went to Molly. "I would like to see you dance," he said, wiggling his eyebrows.

His eyes said so much more—that he would like to see her dance *naked*. For him.

A knock came at the door, and even before she turned, Molly saw the zest and pleasure drain from Alejandro's face, caught a quick look of terror on Josefina's face before she reached for her uncle's hand.

The sheriff, Kenny Wagner, an Anglo in his forties, stood there, a slightly apologetic expression in his eyes as he looked at Molly. Her heart clutched, hard.

"Alejandro Sosa?" he asked.

"Yes," Alejandro said, putting down his guitar cautiously.

"We need to talk." Wagner shot a glance toward Josefina. "Outside here if you wouldn't mind."

Josefina screamed and clutched her uncle's hand. "No! You can't go!"

Alejandro kissed her, disentangled his hand as gently as he was able. "I will be right back," he said. "Promise."

Josefina looked at Molly. "Help him!"

She nodded, her throat too tight for words. In the hallway, she pulled the door tight and said harshly, "What's going on?"

"Sorry, Molly," the sheriff said soberly. "I...uh... had a tip that I needed to talk to your friend here."

"A tip," she echoed bitterly. "I can just imagine where it came from."

He had the grace to look abashed. "Yeah. Well. I gotta uphold the law."

Molly glanced at Alejandro, and saw that his face was set in grim, sharp lines.

Instinctively, Molly moved to take Alejandro's hand. "Kenny, he's not my friend. He's my husband." She lifted her chin. "We were married two days ago."

Kenny looked down. "So I heard." He pursed his lips. "You may not be aware that the laws governing immigration have changed somewhat in recent years."

Alejandro's hand tightened on Molly's, and with a pain in her chest, she said, "In what way?"

"It doesn't matter if you're married. He has to go back and apply for permission, just the same as everyone else."

"But...! That's impossible! He can't!" As if to hold him here, Molly gripped Alejandro's arm, suddenly aware of the warm scent of his skin. "I love him."

"I'm sorry."

"No!" The word was as fierce as any utterance she'd made in all her life. Wildly, she searched her memory for something, anything that might help.

Alejandro said gently, his hand on her back, "Molly, it will be all right."

"No," she said again, and found herself very near tears.

In a rush, Molly said, "You can't take him. He's setting up my farm for me. No one else can do the work the way I want it."

"Molly, don't make this harder, all right? I'm willing to cut some slack here if you cooperate, but if you draw some line in the sand, you're going to tie my hands, understand?''

''No, I don't understand. What do you mean, slack?''

''I'll let him stay till the little girl is out of the hospital if you'll agree he goes home then and applies for legal entry.'' He looked at Alejandro.

''But my farm! We've made plans!'' She couldn't seem to remember what they were and her words stuttered and stopped as she struggled with them. ''He's...drawing. And there will be roosters.''

The sheriff smiled over her head. ''Not more than one, I hope.''

''No,'' Alejandro said, amusement in his voice. ''Only one.''

Molly looked up at him and found him smiling. Didn't he understand how serious this was?

''You see why she needs help to make a farm.''

Her heart was pounding so hard she could barely hear. ''Yes, you see, I can't do it myself.''

''I understand that.'' His lips worked. ''Fact is, though, the law says he can only stay here to do a job if there's no one else to do it. Plenty of folks could help you set up a farm.''

''But—''

The blue eyes, usually so genial, went hard. ''Take it or leave it, Molly. If you want to make it rough, we can go that road.''

''No, sir,'' Alejandro said, his hands on Molly's shoulders. ''Thank you.''

They shook hands, an act that, for some reason, made Molly completely crazy. What was there to be friendly about? Still, she held her peace until the sheriff put his hat back on and left them.

"Why did you agree?" she asked.

The affability was gone. "There was no choice. You do not want to be arrested. I do not wish to go until Josefina is better." His expression was grim. "This has been too much trouble for you. For that, I am sorry."

"It hasn't—"

From the room came Josefina's cry. Alejandro held up a finger. "Let me comfort her. I will be right back."

"No, stay with her. I have something I need to do."

"Molly—"

"It won't hurt you or me, I promise. I'm going to see my brother."

"He is only acting as he feels is best for you."

"No," she said bitterly. "You're wrong about that."

Filled with a sense of betrayal, she stopped first at the station, but the woman behind the desk told Molly that Josh was out.

"Out? Do you have any idea where?" Molly said with veiled impatience, knowing the woman knew exactly where the deputies were at any given moment. "I really need to see him."

The woman languorously wheeled her chair from her computer to a log on the desk. Blinking prettily, she said, "Sorry, Molly. I don't show a location."

Molly bit back a retort, took a breath and said, "Thank you."

Glancing at her watch, she saw it was midafternoon. Josh might have stopped off to get a late lunch. She stopped at the Navajo Café and hopped up on a stool at the counter, glad to see a familiar face. "Hi, Maureen," she said to the waitress. "Have you seen my brother today?"

Maureen didn't look up from her task of dividing a

pie into serving sizes. Molly leaned forward, half smiling. ''Maureen? Are you daydreaming?''

The woman looked up, met Molly's eyes and kept cutting.

Molly bit her lip, tried one more time. ''May I have a cup of coffee, please?''

The waitress put down her knife, stalked over to the coffeemaker, poured a cup neatly and settled it in front of Molly, all without a word. She went back to her pie, put it in the safe and went into the kitchen to fetch an order.

Molly's heart felt as if someone were stepping on it. Sipping coffee, she glanced over her shoulder at the sparse, midafternoon crowd, and was surprised by an expression of dislike on a woman's face. Tiny Moran, in her flowered dresses, had taught Sunday school to Molly as a girl, brought her treats when she was sick. Before Molly could wave or smile, Mrs. Moran looked away.

Turning back to her coffee, Molly had the sense she'd broken some code she'd barely been aware existed.

Behind her, someone laughed, and Molly found herself cringing a little, wondering what they were saying about her. It wasn't that hard to imagine. No doubt Alejandro's good looks had been discussed in detail, and there were bound to be comments about an irascible charmer using the gullible widow to get a green card.

Not all of it would be mean-spirited. They were not, in general, a mean-spirited bunch. They were ruggedly individualistic, as well, forged in the live-and-let-live world of the West. In no time, they would begin to sympathize with the plight of a man who needed to care for a little girl who depended on him—all of them could relate to that, and because extended families were often so large and so common, there would be little distinction made between a niece and a daughter. Soon, everyone would forget that he had come to them an outsider. His charm, his good looks, his devotion to his duty would all win approval for him. The women would lead it.

How well she knew them! And in that moment of honesty, she could admit that she had not broken some vague community code she'd known nothing about. She had known, right from the beginning, that she was risking their censure if they discovered what she'd done. More, she'd done it willfully, and everyone knew it now.

Her crime was not one of passion. They would have forgiven passion. No, her crime was much more basic: she'd lied.

She'd lied when she found him—lied to her brother about Josefina visiting her, lied to her doctor and the pharmacist about a nonexistent sore throat, lied to her boss about being sick. And lied some more by saying she was in love with a man only so he could get a green card.

Lied, and they all knew it. Her punishment would be a form of banishment, an exclusion from their ranks that would last until she had had time to win back their trust. In some cases, it was likely gone forever. With the rest, it would take quite a while.

Maureen sailed by with the coffeepot and topped off Molly's coffee and bolted away before Molly could say anything. Which, now that she understood the lay of the land, she would not.

She had known what consequences she had risked

by undertaking this business, and thinking of Alejandro, lying almost dead on her land that morning, she knew she would do exactly the same thing all over again. Her actions had saved a little girl's life, and even if she could, she wouldn't do anything to change that.

Still, it was with a vague sense of loss that she took two one-dollar bills from her purse and put them on the counter for the coffee and a tip and left, as an outsider would, without stopping to chat with anyone.

On the sidewalk, the wind sailed around the corner of the building and slammed into her body, ice-cold. Surprised, she lifted her head and scented moisture in the air, and to the west was a line of dark gray clouds, low and heavy. There would be snow before morning—and right on time.

She still needed to find her brother. But just now, she had lost heart.

Alejandro sat with Josefina until she was calm again, and fell asleep, then remembered he had promised to keep his strength up, and went to the cafeteria for a meal.

As he sat there, the pretty nurse from Molly's floor came in. Spying Alejandro, she made a beeline to him. "Hi. Are you okay?"

He nodded, and glanced around, unwilling to give the wrong impression. "Yes, thank you." He went back to his food.

"Do you mind if I sit down for a minute?"

He had no wish to be rude, but he had not missed her flirtatious glances before, and perhaps someone would think the wrong thing. As he tried to think how to answer her, she smiled. "Don't worry. It's not the same here. No one will think anything if I sit with you.'' She smiled at his hesitation. ''Promise.''

With a gesture, he indicated the place across from him.

''I couldn't help overhearing what happened in the hallway this afternoon,'' she said. ''And, uh, I want to tell you that they're lying.''

He raised his head. ''Who is lying?''

''The sheriff. And Molly's brother.'' Her large eyes were grave. ''I don't know what the law is exactly, but my cousin married a guy from Mexico and he has a green card, not trouble.'' She shrugged. ''They're just trying to scare you guys.''

Alejandro put down his fork, narrowing his eyes. ''So they cannot make me go.''

The woman sighed, tapping her nail against the table. ''I'm not sure, exactly. They could cook something up, trying to hurt you. If they actually deport you, it might be really hard to get back.''

''Ah.'' He tore a section of tortilla. ''What happens to Molly if I do not let them deport me? Can she be in trouble?''

''Not really.'' She made a sad little face. ''No more than she's in already.''

''She is in trouble now?''

''Not law trouble,'' she said matter-of-factly. ''Just town trouble. Nobody is talking to her.''

He made a face. ''They are making her the outsider.''

''Right. It would be easier for her if she wasn't an Anglo. If her brother wasn't a deputy sheriff, if her husband wasn't a guy—'' She broke off. ''Sorry. I sound like I'm trying to make trouble between you, and although I think she's a very lucky woman, I'm really not like that." She started to stand up. "Sorry."

"Annie, is it?"

"Yes."

"Please, stay a little." He frowned, gesturing her into place. She settled uneasily, her palms flat on the table. "I did not know all these things," he said. "I understand about her brother. And if she were Latina, like you, there would be a place for us, no?"

She nodded.

"But I do not know about her husband. Why does he make it harder for her?"

Annie took a breath, let it go. "Because everybody loved him. He was good people. He was handsome, and real strong, and nice to everybody. If you had trouble, he'd give you the shirt off his back." She warmed to the story, leaned forward. "One time? My grandpa's roof caved in on one side in the snow, and it was Tim who went there and fixed it for nothing."

"I thought," Alejandro said slowly, "that he must have been a very good man to have won Molly."

"Oh my God!" She put a hand over her mouth. "This *is* a green card wedding! I should have guessed! It's just like her to do something like this, and really, it seemed kinda weird that she was just all of a sudden in love so fast—!" She winced. "Sorry."

He shook his head. "I do not wish to cause her problems. She has been very kind to me. To us. My niece would have died if Molly…" He took a breath and blinked at the stab in his side. "I must let her go. There must be something. Some way?"

"Are you sure that's what she wants?"

"No." He raised his head, very sure. "She will wish to continue this marriage, because she thinks it is the best thing for us. But she will lose her brother. Her community. The price is too high.''

Troubled, Annie frowned. ''Do you want me to see what I can find out?''

''Please. And please do not tell Molly that her brother lied to her. There is enough trouble between them. She does not need to know.''

Molly stopped by the grocery store and found the place crowded as all the other locals stocked up in case of a nasty snowfall. Often they came at this time of year, huge snowfalls that stopped everything in the high valley while it came down, stilling the world with a fuzzy whiteout.

She got the groceries, including one full bag for Lynette, who hated driving in the snow. At her brother's house, she saw the cruiser was parked in front, and she carried the bag of groceries to the door, feeling a strange sense of awkwardness. Unbelonging.

A feeling that was not improved when Josh himself opened the door and stepped out onto the porch, putting on his hat in preparation for returning to work. He looked a little startled when he saw her, then remembered to frown. ''We have plenty of groceries, Molly. We're not some charity.''

''You can pay me for them if you think you need to. I wasn't doing it to help you, but your wife.''

''She doesn't need you.''

''And neither do you, right?'' Molly said. She'd meant the words to be angry, bitter, but to her horror, they came attached with the edge of tears in her throat.

He bowed his head, and Molly found her eyes on the tender nape of his neck, below the close bristles of blond hair. It was a vulnerable place, one that showed his youth and stubbornness. "Josh, I hate this so much! You're the only family I have, and I can't stand for us to be in a fight."

For a long minute, he kept his head down, then looked at her, his defenses firmly in place. "We're not in a fight, Moll. We're just on different sides of an issue."

"So it's going to ruin our relationship if I hold an opinion that differs from yours? Is that what's happening here?"

Lynette pulled open the door, scowling. "You two come in here right now," she said in a tone of voice that had been ordering around children for years. "You're not gonna stand on my front porch and air your dirty laundry." When both Josh and Molly hesitated, she put a hand on her hip. "Inside. Now."

They obeyed. Lynette pushed them to the kitchen, thanked Molly for the groceries and put them on the counter, before she bustled toward the door. At the threshold, she paused. "Thrash it out pretty quick. The kids'll be home in a half hour, and I won't have them see you two fighting."

Molly leaned on the counter. "The sheriff stopped by the hospital a little while ago."

Josh sat and took off his hat. A lock of hair stuck up, and Molly ached to smooth it down as she always had. She put her hands in her pockets and waited for him to speak. "I figured," he said.

"Why did you have to do it like that, Josh?"

"I had to, Molly. You're breaking the law. I know that wedding isn't real."

She opened her mouth to lie, then closed it. Maybe the time for lying was over. She thought of Alejandro's hands on her body this morning, thought of his mouth, kissing hers and said instead, "My feelings are very complicated right now, but it doesn't matter anyway. A wedding isn't enough to keep him here." Tears suddenly filled her eyes and she collapsed in the opposite chair. "And it didn't have to come to that. You didn't have to tell them."

An odd expression crossed his face—guilty and confused. "I don't know what you're talking about."

She raised her head, dashing tears away. "All I know is what the sheriff told me—he'll let Alejandro stay until Josefina is out of the hospital, but then he has to go back to Mexico and petition to come back as my husband."

"I'm real sorry, Moll," he said, not sounding sorry at all, "but you're the one who got all noble, not me."

"Noble? There's a lot involved here, but nobility isn't really a big part of it."

Josh sighed. "Moll, don't take this wrong, but—maybe you do like him. Maybe you really want somebody in your life. I can understand that. But did you ever consider that he might be using you?"

"No. He wouldn't do that."

"Cripes, Molly! Listen to yourself! D'you think all those confidence men out there bilking old ladies of their savings are ugly swines who can't string a sentence together? You think that would work?" His blue eyes threw sparks. "This Sosa is real smooth. You should hear the women, all over town, who've seen him. It's like we have some big-time movie star in town. He could have love slaves from here to Mexico City with the snap of a finger."

Molly made a sound of exasperation. "So if a man is charming and good-looking, he's automatically running a con?"

"No! But look at it from his side. Here's this lonely widow, with all that land, no man. How hard would it be?"

"It would be easy," she said, surprisingly calm. "Except that's just not his style."

He rolled his eyes. "Whatever. You aren't going to listen to me, but I'm not going to sit idly by and let you make a fool of yourself with this guy. What happens in six months or a year down the line when he starts sampling the wares of all the women in town?"

"Listen to yourself! You're acting like I'm a sixteen-year-old girl in heat! Like I have no judgment, like I can't make decisions for myself!" She narrowed her eyes. "I don't want to be protected, Josh. I want to live my life on my own terms—and I'll take my chances on making mistakes."

"Fine, but do you have to start by falling in love with some—"

"What, Josh?"

His mouth hardened. "With a guy whose got nothing to lose by taking you for all you have."

"No, damn it! Don't you get it? It might not be a mistake at all! Any more than buying that old house I wanted when I married Tim. I would have been happy in that house, and you know what? If you'd stayed out of my way and let me buy it when Tim died, I would never have met Alejandro."

"What the hell does that have to do with anything? You're not even rational!"

She flung up her hands. "You know what, Josh? You are not hearing one word I'm saying. I love you. You're my brother and I don't want us to be estranged, but if you insist on meddling in my life this way, I'm finished with you. I'm a grown woman. I raised my little brother when our parents died, and saw him safely married. I've been to college and buried a husband. I've lived alone and managed to thrive in spite of everything.'' She shook her head. ''Stay out of my affairs.''

He didn't stop her when she left.

Chapter 12

Alejandro went back to Josefina's room to wait for Molly. When his niece stirred, he played her a soft lullaby, singing softly as he strummed the gentle chords. She was soothed into sleep.

He set the guitar aside and stared out the window, watching dark fall and the wind whip into a fierceness that would bring winter with it. Leaves and dirt spun into whirlwinds, and somewhere out of sight, an empty can clanged over the blacktop. The sound was lonely.

His thoughts whirled like the leaves outside, and he felt dizzy, thinking of how much had changed in such a short time. It was as disorienting as when his sister died, two years ago. One day, he'd been bargaining with a food exporter about the price of his cauliflower. The next, he'd been bargaining with a coyote to shuttle him across the border to take care of Josefina.

Since then, his life had taken on a certain sameness. He'd hated it, all of it—the shacks that passed for living quarters in many places. The haphazard way Josefina went to school. Until his sister died, he'd been very rooted to one place, one lifestyle. Ever since, he'd been as rootless as a tumbleweed.

And now, his situation had become very complicated. This wedding had seemed like an answered prayer. But he could not bear to make life so hard for Molly.

She had already given a hundred times more than most people in her situation. Thanks to her, Josefina was safe and warm in a hospital bed with an illness that could be treated now that they finally knew what it was. Thanks to Molly, Alejandro was not sick in some jail, maybe facing the loss of his leg, but clean and well fed and nearly back to his usual self.

It struck him again—what had made her do this kind thing? Had God or some angel simply been watching over him and Josefina to let such a thing happen?

A tight knot of emotion grew in his chest, anxiety and sorrow and regret. He thought of Molly, of her light-struck eyes so pure and clear when he kissed her ring at the wedding. Looking at his own ring, he frowned. They were married, and it had been consummated. He should not have let himself make love to her this morning. He had known, even as he reached for her, that it was wrong—that it sealed the vow they had made, and more than that, it caused risk for her.

And yet, thinking of her now, of the way she stood in her kitchen, so achingly vulnerable, almost bold in her robe with nothing beneath it, he knew he could never have walked away. He had been longing to touch her for days, and all through the night, when her warmth and woman smell had been so close, it had been a piercing sort of torture. He'd managed to keep himself aloof then, but that glimpse of her naked breast, just the delicate upper swell, offered and not offered, had been too much to resist. Too much for his lust, and too much for his heart.

For in that moment, she had needed him. At last. Needed something he alone could give her—the touch of a man for her lonely skin, the kiss of desire for her hungry mouth, the devotion only he, with his snared heart, could give to heal her long, long hurt.

But had he given or taken?

He closed his eyes, remembering the taste of her. The look of her throat while she rode him, the lift of her small, pretty breasts that fit exactly into the nest of his hand, the nipples rising to kiss his palms. Oh, yes, he had taken much with him today.

And yet, in his madness, he had not thought of protecting her. They had used nothing. If she became pregnant...

"Madre," he whispered to the glass, bowing his head. The idea made him ache with longing. He would like to see her with his child. He wished it could be so, that this could be a true marriage. They had only known each other a short time, but it did not seem to matter to his heart.

He looked at his niece, seeing her thinness and the paleness of her cheeks and he wondered suddenly if he had done her a disservice. If he had not dedicated himself to satisfying his sister's foolish preference for America, Josefina would not even be sick at all. She would be sleeping now in a cozy bed, her skin brown from her play and chores outside. She would have many cousins and uncles and aunts to love her, instead of only Alejandro.

But now it was too late for that. She had to remain

until her illness was cured. Then he would return to Mexico, return to what he knew and people he loved. Suddenly, he was so weary of this country that he wanted to weep.

Somehow, he would let Molly go. Somehow, he would stay here with Josefina.

And somehow, he would have to keep his heart from shattering when he saw his saint every day, not thinking of him at all while she moved in her world, a world in which he had no place.

Molly picked up Alejandro and drove back to the house. Neither of them spoke much, but when they went inside, they both moved to the kitchen, wordless. He reached for the teapot to boil water. Molly reached for the coffeepot. They stopped, both smiling as they reached the sink, and there was one split second in which Molly knew she could turn back, one minute when she could have halted everything.

She didn't. Instead, when he reached for her, she was reaching back, and they were somehow kissing, the kind of wild, openmouthed and desperate kiss that spoke of a hunger that should have been somewhat appeased by their morning in bed together.

But all Molly could think was that she needed him even more now, that if she was going to lose him again so fast she had to make the best of the time they had.

And this time, she drew him past the open door to the back room and took him into her room, and it was there that they made love, first with a kind of driven frenzy that was graceless and pointed, completed before they even managed to get half their clothing off. Then again, gently, slowly, taking time to know where to kiss, to stroke, to linger and to tease.

This time, there was no pressing obligation to make them rise, and they lay together, sated, her belly and breasts pressed into his side, his arm looped around her neck.

After a time, Alejandro turned on his side and slid down so they were lying face-to-face. He touched her cheek. "I told myself we should not do this again."

Molly blinked lazily, her body tingling and relieved. "I'm glad you didn't stick to it."

He grinned. "Me, too." He stroked her shoulder, touched her elbow, and his face sobered. "But I worry, Molly, that I will leave you with a child."

She shook her head. "Don't. There's always a chance, of course, but I tried for a long time to conceive with my husband, and we were not blessed with children."

"You wanted them?"

"Oh, yes. A houseful."

"And are there no children for women to take in here?"

Molly almost said no. But that wasn't strictly true. There were plenty of children who did not have homes. Older children or those of mixed race. "My husband was not interested in adopting, particularly. We thought we'd just keep trying." Her gaze fell to his chest and she put a hand on it, open, right over his heart. "Did you ever marry?"

"No." His lashes fell, hiding his eyes. "I had been thinking of it some when my sister died, but until then, I was very busy with the farm."

"Thinking of someone in particular?" she asked, envisioning a woman with long dark hair, busty and slim-hipped. It gave her a strange pang.

"Two of them." A glint came in his eyes, as if he

sensed her jealousy. "There were twenty or more who would have gladly wed me, of course."

Molly smiled. "Twenty? All for your good looks?"

He snorted lightly. "For my strong back, and my good head for figures and the land my uncle and I made profitable." He shifted, and more seriously said, "It isn't so much beauty, eh? A man who will take care of his family, that's to be valued."

"Yes," she said soberly. "It is." And it seemed, suddenly, a very great tragedy that circumstances should have robbed his hometown or village or whatever it was, of such a man as Alejandro Sosa, who would have been a good husband and a good father and good provider, who had love in him and honor, and energy to make things happen. Some woman who had lived in that village all those years, maybe looking at him from the corner of her eye, measuring his fit to her life, had lost a very good husband. "Do you miss it?"

He was silent, and in the reflection of the lamp on his dark irises, she thought she could see memories moving. Finally, he looked at her. "Yes. But this is what I have been given to do." A slight lift of a shoulder. "Be a father to Josefina. That is more important."

She kissed him then. Closed her eyes and kissed him and breathed in the smell of his skin, and pressed her body close to his, knowing she would never meet another man like him again.

It was snowing when they arose much later, both very hungry. They raced to the kitchen, laughing, and Alejandro halted, the saucepan he used to make coffee still in his hand, staring out the window.

"Oh," he sighed, an expression of perfect wonderment. "Look, Molly! It's so beautiful." He walked to the long glass door and pushed aside the drapes to see more of it, thick swirls of snow chasing each other, sparkling against the light from the kitchen, everything awash in it. "Josefina will be so happy—she has not seen it snow very often." He glanced at her over his shoulder. "Usually, we are gone by the time the snows come."

"I love snow," she said, and leaned on the counter, her hair scattering over her shoulders as she peered out at it. And it seemed to Alejandro that winter was reflected in those pale eyes. In her bare feet and oversize robe, he thought she, too, was very beautiful. "I used to wait and wait and wait for the first snow." She laughed softly, watching as he measured coffee and water and turned on the heat under the pot. As if it spurred her on, she opened the fridge and started arranging a plate with paper-thin slices of roast beef, and olives, and sliced tomatoes. He plucked them off as she arranged them.

She smiled and carried what was left on the tray to the table. He joined her, and made a sandwich, feeling a taste in his mouth he couldn't quite name. The cold night and the smell of coffee and making love made him want—something besides bland American meats. He ate because he was hungry, but he told himself tomorrow he would find something with bite to it. It had been many days since he'd tasted anything... normal.

But here, this was normal. The thought reminded him that this was not his world. Sobering a little, he said, "Did you find your brother today?"

Her face closed so tightly, so completely that she didn't have to say it had not gone well. She plucked crust from her sandwich and nodded. He waited for her to speak, but she seemed intent on keeping her eyes lowered. Her mouth grew taut, and he said finally, "Was it so terrible, Molly?"

She lifted her head. "He's my only family. I wanted to see if we could make it right between us. He wouldn't listen to me, and that makes me sad. It also made me very angry. He doesn't understand," she said. "He wants to make all my decisions and mistakes for me."

Mistakes. Would she look back five years from now, ten, and think this time had been a mistake? He hoped not, hoped that he could leave her with some legacy that would make her very glad she'd helped him.

She went to a cupboard and took out a large sketch-pad, carried it to the table and flipped back the first few pages, so quickly he could not see what was on them, to reveal a watercolor painting of a house.

"Is this your work?"

She nodded.

Alejandro touched the page lightly with his fingers, surprised by what the spare, soft lines made him feel—a sense of yearning and a certain lost hope that seemed to come from the yawning, obviously empty windows. "It's very good. You do not want to spoil this with hard lines, as you asked me to show you. This is different."

"So soft. That's what my art teachers used to tell me. That it was too soft, that I needed more definition." She brushed the subject away with a fling of her fingers. "Anyway, this house is here in town." She flipped another page, and another, showing him different views of it—one at night, all lit up with a family in the windows. Another made it the haunted house of a ghost story.

''I fell in love with this house when I was about nine years old. An old woman lived there and she used to let me pick lilacs and roses and whatever I wanted, as long as I asked her first, so I wouldn't take her special favorites.''

He grinned. ''I like such a woman.''

''Me, too.'' A finger traced the edge of the page. ''This is what it looks like now. It's been condemned. Nobody wants to take the time to fix it up and nobody has bothered to tear it down, so it sits there, all lonely and sad.'' Musingly, she said, *''Aislado.''*

He looked from the drawing to her face. ''You wanted it.''

She nodded. ''It came up for sale when my husband and I got married. He didn't want to mess with it—too much work.'' She gave him a little wry smile. ''And like you, he was land crazy. Just had to have land.''

Alejandro thought of her resistance to his vision for the ways her land could be used to make her self-sufficient, and with some surprise realized that it was not everyone's wish to have land to work. ''Did your husband work the land?''

She shook her head. ''He was going to start the following spring. He'd been saving for it a long time, to buy the equipment and seed and topsoil.'' She lifted a shoulder. ''When he died, I wanted to buy it anyway, with some of the insurance money. It seemed like a good investment, and I thought he would be glad…'' She faltered a little, staring hard at the page. She took a breath and raised her eyes. ''Glad to have me do something that would take away some of my sorrow.'' She shook her head. ''My brother threw a fit. He missed Tim, you know. It really upset him when he died—and he just thought I was awful for wanting to buy the house. He wanted me to put the money into the land, make a farm, when I never even wanted that!''

Alejandro's heart sank. The one thing he could give she did not want. To hide his disappointment, he took her hand, spoke encouragingly. ''And you allowed him to change your mind.''

''Sort of. I didn't do the farm, but I didn't buy the house either. Ever since I've been living in a frozen world, where nothing changes.'' She sat on the chair opposite him and touched his face. ''I don't know why I had to bring you into my house, Alejandro, and I don't know where it will lead, for either of us. But this time, I know I'm right, and I'm not going to let him— or any of the rest of the people who tried today—bully me out of it.''

''Others?''

She rolled her eyes, straightening to flip her sketch-book closed. Hiding. ''Don't worry about it. It's a small town. I'm sure you know what that's like.''

Yes. He did know. He knew that memories were long and often punishing, that small minds sometimes held the greatest sway. ''Molly, I cannot allow you to—''

She raised an eyebrow. ''Can't allow?''

''That's not what I meant. I do not want to give you sorrow, not after all you've done for us. I hate that my coming brought you trouble.''

To his surprise, she smiled. ''I don't. For the first time in years, I feel really alive.''

That might be so. Perhaps that was the legacy he would leave her. Still, the situation reinforced his growing sense that he had to find another way to stay here with Josefina. He had to set Molly free to forget this little dream time and go on with the life she was meant to live. Quietly, he said, "I will miss you when I have to go, Molly. But maybe it's best this way, you know?"

She gave him that bright, fake smile he'd grown to understand hid her deepest wounds. "Maybe. Everyone knows it was a green-card wedding anyway."

He frowned. "Molly, if I do not understand, you must tell me."

"You understand," she said. "Once you leave for a while, the people in town will see Josefina and like her, and they'll start thinking of me as a hero. And when you come back and we're divorced, no one will think it's strange—a quick meeting, then a difference of opinion when our passion cooled." She lifted one stiff shoulder. "They'll stop gossiping and my brother will come to dinner at my house again."

Alejandro struggled with the knowledge Annie had given him, that the threat from the sheriff was a lie. That the wedding was enough to secure his green card. His wish to stay in her home, prove to her that he had something to give, warred with the certainty that his presence had made her life very difficult.

She stood and put the drawing pad back in the closet, leaving him wondering how to ease by those walls and discover what was really in her mind. Did she wish for him to stay? It seemed the highest arrogance for him to think so, when she had never uttered words of fondness for him, had even wept in his arms for her lost husband.

He bowed his head for a moment, thinking. In his own world, what would he have done, thought? But it was too hard to imagine. There, where work and family and tradition were the cornerstones of life, Alejandro was a good choice for a husband. He would not ever grow rich, especially in American terms, but his life would be solid, fairly secure. At home, he had much to offer.

Here, he had nothing but the soft talent of guitar and his strong back. No money, no standing, a place only as an outsider whose appearance in her life had dragged her outside, too. His pride would not let him offer himself until he had more to give.

But he found he was not strong enough to stay away from her now, in the quiet of a snowy night, with hurt lying on her spine. He rose and put his arms around her small body, pulling her close. For now he would use his hands and his mouth and his laughter to ease the sorrow she still carried.

Feeling her melt closer into him, he closed his eyes and summoned the right notes of desire for her to hear in his voice. "Tonight we have a big warm bed, hmm?" he said. "Let's use it well."

She turned, urgently, and put her hands on him. "Let's do," she said, and laughed as his hands opened her robe, laughed throatily as she pressed her breasts and hips into him.

Chapter 13

Molly and Alejandro went to the hospital after breakfast. In the brilliant, snow-washed morning, it seemed they should both be cloaked in a gilded, new-lovers' glow, but that wasn't what Molly felt at all. She felt dread. Worry.

And worst of all, a doomed sense of her own impending broken heart. It had been very, very foolish to let herself fall in love with a man from another world, one so very distant from her own. And yet, she had.

He held open the door for her, and she looked up at his face, that face she had almost recognized when she'd seen it the very first time, a face that was now carved irrevocably upon her heart. For one tiny moment, he paused, those dark eyes full of light and gentleness and strength, then he was gesturing for her to proceed him.

He waved at the nurses jauntily. Annie called them over. "I have some good news for you," Annie said.

"Dr. Indira is waiting for you in her office. She asked me to tell you to come see her when you got here."

Alejandro looked at Molly and she caught a wild flare of emotion in his eyes. For a moment, she thought he was going to reach for her hand, but then he was standing straight and leading the way down the hall.

"Good morning, Mr. Sosa," Dr. Indira said, smiling broadly. "Hi, Molly. I have great news for both of you—Josefina is out of the woods. I'd like her to stay overnight, but there's no reason in the world that you can't take her home tomorrow."

A swoop of emotion went through Molly. Joy and sorrow, mixed together. How would this change things? "Tomorrow?"

"If you weren't a nurse, I might keep her for a few days, but you're familiar enough with procedures that I don't have to worry about her. The pneumonia is clearing, and you can keep her isolated from others until the TB comes back clean, right?"

"Yes!" Her tongue felt swollen in her mouth, but she managed to inject some confidence into her voice. "I know the drill perfectly, and it would be so much healthier for her to be home."

Only then did she glance at Alejandro and see the troubled expression on his face.

So did the doctor. "Are you worried about her, Mr. Sosa?"

"No." He seemed to come from a place far away, and shook his head. "No, this is very good." He looked at Molly. "Let's tell her."

In the hall, he stepped out of the traffic flow and took her arm, drawing her next to him, putting his hand around her shoulders, and Molly felt an almost painful swell of emotion. "What will we do now, my saint?"

he whispered. His breath was warm and moist against her hair. "Will you care for her in your home?"

She raised her head, realizing how selfish she'd been. Alejandro wasn't thinking of them at all, but of Josefina and her safety. "Of course, Alejandro! Whatever else happens, you can trust me. I'll take very good care of her."

He swallowed. "I know."

He cocked his head down the hall. A wash of whitish light glossed his hair as he did it, and Molly thought, *even this is beautiful.* "Let's tell Josefina."

Alejandro felt as if he were dragging a bag of rocks behind him as they spoke with Josefina. He kept his mask carefully neutral, but the moment had arrived. Now he would have to let Molly go.

Let her go. Even the words caused a deep echo of protest to stir in his guts, but he knew it was the only choice. He'd seen too clearly how much she missed her brother, how much it pained her to be ignored by the people of the town. If he did not release her now, she would resent him one day.

That he could not bear.

He mentally rehearsed his plan. She would protest, and he thought carefully how to counter that, in terms with which she could not argue.

And suddenly, he sympathized with her brother, Josh, worrying over her goodness and generosity of spirit. Taking Alejandro into her house might have been a very dangerous act, something her brother knew very clearly, working as he did with the law. Alejandro might have been anyone, of any sort of character. He might have hurt Molly.

And though he believed his character was strong,

Alejandro was going to hurt her now—to save them both pain later. He mourned that. Mourned that she might think he had only made love to her in a casual way, that he took lovers as easily as many of the men he knew. Mourned that even their easy friendship would have to be sacrificed.

But it was necessary. To preserve and restore her reputation, Alejandro would have to pretend to believe her brother's lie, return to Mexico. Josefina could heal a little. Maybe then, he could come get her, take her back with him. And leave Molly to repair her life and make peace with the husband she still mourned, though she did not admit it.

He loved her. And love, as his mother told him often enough, was not selfish or grasping. Love served.

Alejandro would serve her best by letting her go.

Outside the hospital, Alejandro halted. "Molly, you must listen."

A faint, apprehensive frown. "What is it?"

"When Josefina comes to your house, I will stay a day or two, then return to Mexico." He touched her arm. "Not for me. For you. Annie told me what the town is doing to you." He paused. "She also told me it is a lie, that the green-card wedding is not enough. So I will go home for a few days, come back—and maybe you can just say—" a shrug "—that it is too much, the little girl and me and the dog."

"Alejandro—"

He put his fingers over her mouth. "This is best."

"Is it?"

"Listen." He took her hands. "You must, to be happy, make peace with your brother and your people here. To give you that chance, I must not live under your roof.''

''Stop being so damned noble, will you?'' She tugged out of his grasp. ''If you want to go, just go. Stop giving me these weird excuses.''

His eyes narrowed sharply. ''You are too stubborn to see what I see. That you need your family. Your town. You have been very unhappy with them looking at you, talking about you behind your back.''

And damn him, he was right. She hated this, hated feeling as if she'd been banished in some arcane tribal ritual. And in time, she would resent him. She crossed her arms, feeling genuine grief well up in her heart. ''At least let Josefina stay with me until she's better. Will you let me do that much?''

''How can you, Molly? You have work. You have friends.'' He shook his head, smiling softly. ''I thought I should make your land give you its bounty, to pay my debt to you. What I see now is that God sent me to you, just as you were sent to me, so we could both have better lives now. You have been frozen, as you said last night. I have been lost.''

She found she had a smile, a very sad one, in her after all. ''You thawed me out, all right.''

''And you found me a place to call home.'' He looked away and Molly sensed, suddenly, that it was as hard for him to walk away as it was for her to let him. ''We will be friends. Later, when it is not so hard. Okay?''

Tears burned in her throat, burned so hot she wanted to scream them away. She closed her eyes and willed them away. ''Okay.''

And as if he could not resist, he stepped forward and pulled her into a deep, close, rib-crushing embrace for a long minute, then kissed her head and let her go. "We should make arrangements today, for my niece. Tonight, call your brother and have him come to dinner. I will cook for him, and we will tell him the truth."

Molly nodded. But she wondered which version of truth they would present.

As she drove toward the ranch, Alejandro said suddenly, "Your house, the one you draw so much, is it around here somewhere?"

"Not far." She smiled, attempting a normal expression. "It isn't like anything is far from anything else around here."

"Will you show it to me?"

Molly shrugged. "Sure, I guess." She changed lanes and turned left, into the oldest part of town. Much of it was shabby, but the lots were generous and flanked with winter-bare elms and poplars and cottonwoods that made a tunnel of shade in summer. Molly parked on the street. "There it is."

"Can we get out? Look in the windows?"

"Why?"

He shrugged. "I want to see what captured you."

He sounded as though he meant it, and they got out, crunching over leaves and snow in the late afternoon. More clouds had rolled in, and they lent a lonely aspect to the neglected house. She tried to see it with fresh eyes, taking in the peeling paint, the faded gingerbread, the boarded windows.

But instead, she snagged on the same things that always caught her. The leaded glass windows on the first floor, the eyebrow window in the roof, the long, wide porch that circled the front and both sides, ending in a screen door at the side. In memory, she saw it the way it had been in spring, with lilacs blooming from the enormous bushes that ran down one side of the wide lawn. She smiled. "It must seem amazing that this is it."

"No," he said quietly, turning to look at her. "I see your name written on it, Molly, right there, under that window. See?"

She glanced up, half expecting to see her name. Of course it wasn't there. He was teasing her, and she smiled again. "It's really amazing inside. Hardwood floors. Big wide staircase. Six bedrooms!"

He bent to pick up a bedraggled For Sale sign. "Why do you not buy it now?"

A wind skittered over the yard, kicking up leaves and waving the arms of the trees overhead. She pulled a lock of loose hair from her eyes. "I don't have the skills to fix it. I needed Tim for that."

He lifted a shoulder. "He was a good carpenter. But not the only one in the world, eh?"

Molly nodded because he seemed to want agreement. But she looked at the turret with its pointed roof and knew she would never buy the house. And somehow, the thought made her feel winded. Lost.

She shivered and crossed her arms. "I'm freezing. Let's go get this over with."

Chapter 14

Alejandro banished her to the living room while he cooked something mysterious he wouldn't name, with ingredients he'd purchased with his pay from Wiley. Outside, a cold wind blew last night's snow around, and Molly stared at it with a hollow feeling, wishing she were in the kitchen with Alejandro.

Josh and Lynette showed up right on time, without the children, both of them nicely dressed, and Molly smiled, knowing how much they treasured these times alone together. As they came up the walk, Josh said something, a joke by the way Lynette leaned close to him and laughed. Her blond hair blew over his shoulder and he put his arm around her.

Molly had called Josh this afternoon, confessing everything, in return for his help seeing to Josefina's safety. He had agreed with relief. As she unfolded herself to go to the door, she heard a clang from the kitchen, and Alejandro swore, rather strongly, in Spanish. She smiled, thinking he must have burned himself.

And suddenly, she was breathlessly sorry that he was going. That this was an end, instead of a beginning. She had to stop and breathe deeply for a minute before she opened the door and smiled brightly. "Hi! Come on in. It's freezing!"

Josh smiled at her, and held up a six-pack of beer. "Lynette promised to drive us home, so I hope you don't mind if I kick back a few."

"Of course not. I may join you."

Lynette hugged her, and again Molly felt a rush of—something. Love and relief. "I missed you," she said. It had only been a week or so, but it seemed an age.

"Me, too." Her plump arms were tight.

To her amazement, Josh stepped forward, too, and gave her a surprisingly fierce hug. "Sorry, sis."

Molly almost lost it, but there was a step from behind her, and she managed to swallow her tears before she turned. Alejandro, wiping his hands on a towel, had emerged from the kitchen, and Molly gestured, bringing him into the group while she stepped back. "You remember Lynette and Josh."

"Yes. It is good of you to come tonight." He extended his hand, and this time, Josh took it. "Things are nearly finished. Come."

He'd set the table with her pottery bowls, and put them on bright turquoise mats she'd almost forgotten, and he'd gathered candles from various places all over the house to put on the table. They burned brightly amid small bowls of marigolds and a tall thin vase of carnations. She'd never seen her own table look so festive, and when she raised her head to tell him so, she saw him waiting for her reaction, his eyes oddly grave.

"Beautiful."

He held her gaze for one moment more, then looked away quickly, and seemed a little confused over what should be done next, looking at the stove and the counter.

"What can I carry?" Molly asked. A thick stew with what looked like hominy bubbled in a pot. A fragrance of chiles and onion rose from it, and mixed with the scent of cinnamon from the coffee in another pot. Molly inhaled, closing her eyes. "Oh, this is going to be wonderful, Alejandro!" Without thought, she put her hand on his arm and turned to Lynette. "Wait until you taste his coffee. You'll never drink American coffee again."

"No machine coffee," Alejandro said, smiling down at her. He put his hand over hers, squeezed it once and let it go.

Somehow, touching him gave her a sense of strength and the tight knot of loss in her chest eased a little. He might be gone tomorrow, but tonight he was here, and she would not lose whatever memories she could tuck away by mourning the loss in the future. "What is this?" she asked of the stew.

"Posole," he said, and Lynette cried out happily. He grinned over his shoulder. "You like it?"

"I love it," she said, and patted her round tummy. "But then, look at me—I love everything." She laughed to show she didn't mind. "Mainly, though, I really love, love, love Mexican food."

He carried the pot to the table. "Yeah? It's good here. Josefina, my niece, has eaten well in New Mexico. I do my best, but I am not a cook like her mother was." He shrugged, went back to the stove, took a thick package of foil out of the oven and opened it, releasing the steam of an enormous stack of thick flour tortillas. "I had to buy the tortillas. I do not know how to make them very well."

They settled around the table, Molly at one end, Alejandro at the other, the candles and flowers between them. He filled their bowls with his rich stew, and talked lightly of many things, drawing even Josh into the conversation. Molly ate the stew with a pile of tortillas and drank a cold beer with her brother, and felt deeply satisfied. Outside, the wind howled and snow began to fall, but in here, there was family and good food and warmth, and what else did a person need?

Josh stood up to get another beer, and offered one to Alejandro, who shook his head with a smile. "No, thank you." He lifted his chin with a little smile. "Molly will drink mine."

"You don't drink?" His eyes narrowed. "You in AA?"

Alejandro gave Molly a puzzled expression. "Why do people always ask that? Only people who have trouble refuse alcohol here?"

Lynette cracked up, and put her hand on his sleeve. "No, I don't drink either. I just don't like it. You're safe."

"I'll take his, Josh," Molly said. "Don't worry about it—all the more for us, right?"

He nodded and carried the beers back to the table. "How's your niece doing?"

"Very well. They will let her go tomorrow." He pushed his bowl away a little, glanced at Molly, then away. "That is why we are here tonight, since I will be moving in a day or two."

"That's what Molly told me."

There was, suddenly, no point to either woman being

at the table, for the men faced each other, looking each other in the eye. "We are both sorry for lying to you," Alejandro said. "It seemed there was no other way."

Molly quietly stood and began to collect the bowls. Lynette helped her.

"I was only trying to protect her, man," Josh said. "It wasn't personal."

"Sure. I know." Alejandro looked at Molly as she took his dishes, and again, it was as if they entered their own little world when their eyes touched, a place where only the two of them knew the rules. "She is too trusting." He looked back at Josh. "But I am grateful. She saved my life, and the life of my niece. We can never repay our debt to her."

Molly took the bowls to the sink, where Lynette had poured soap and now ran hot water. Lynette looked up at Molly, and widened her eyes, trying to give Molly a message she didn't quite get. She frowned, shaking her head. Lynette pressed her mouth together, looked at the men. Shook her head.

"Now that this is out in the open," Josh said, "I need to know what happened, exactly, if you wouldn't mind." He looked at his sister. "Did you really know the little girl before?"

Molly, the pot of stew in her hands, looked at Alejandro. Hesitated, then shook her head. "I found him at the foot of the bluff the morning after the raid." She put the stew down. "I know they say there are no shots fired, but he had a bullet in his leg and broken ribs— and I couldn't leave him there."

Josh bowed his head. "It was me."

"What was you?"

He lifted his head, and in his too-young face she saw lines of weariness. "I fired that night. Twice. One went by, but I guess the other one—'' He cleared his throat. "So in a weird kind of way, all this was my fault.''

Molly sank into a chair. "Josh, how could you?''

He shook his head. "Don't think I haven't asked myself that same thing a hundred times, every night ever since.'' He rubbed his face. "It was so crazy that night. So many people scattering.'' Josh looked at Molly. "I lost my temper. It just pissed me off that all these people were here, breaking the law. And Wiley just sits up there like a fat cat, pretending he doesn't know they're all illegal.'' His jaw went tight. "And you know, it really is a problem for the county. Crime goes up and the jail is packed, and the hospital fills up, and the county gets stuck with all the bills.'' He looked at Alejandro. "You seem like an all-right guy. I'm sorry for your troubles, but why do you have to be here?''

Molly opened her mouth to interrupt, worried that the conversation was going into dangerous territory. Alejandro lifted a hand, and she understood he wanted to field this.

Earnestly, he put his arms on the table. "I do not wish to be here,'' he said. "I love my home. In Mexico, I am an important man where I live. My family has land and I have the respect of the men I do business with.'' He shook his head. "Here I am nothing.''

"So why do it? Why drag that poor little girl all over?''

"I promised her mother I would take care of her. Josefina was her only child, and my sister wanted to raise her here.''

Josh nodded.

Lynette said, "Molly, will you come with me for a minute?''

Startled, she glanced up, saw the urgent expression and followed her out.

Alejandro watched them go, and when they were out of earshot, he said quietly, "*Señor,* who I am is not important now. I must ask you to do one thing."

"What?"

"You must help your sister buy that house she likes so much, the one in town."

"She told you about that?"

He shrugged. "We talked of many things. It is very important to her, that house, and she thinks she should not have it."

Josh's mouth was serious, his blue eyes troubled. "She can't do the work it needs."

"So, she can hire it to be done." Alejandro tried to think of a way to express the sense he had that Molly had to have the house. "Without something to believe in, something that belongs to only her, she will…" he frowned, thinking of a loaf of bread without its insides "—go hollow. No more of her, only the outside."

"Why do you care?"

Because he loved her. Because he couldn't stand to think of that expression on her face when she looked at it this afternoon, so much longing, so much fear, so much certainty that anything she wanted that much would always be out of reach. But he could not think how to say all of that without revealing his heart, and he only shook his head. "She saved my life."

Josh smiled. "I'll see what I can do, man. Maybe she can sell this place and do what she wants with the house."

Alejandro nodded. "Thank you."

* * *

Lynette hustled Molly into the bedroom and closed the door, then leaned against it. "You want to tell me what's going on here?" she said.

Molly frowned. "What do you mean?"

"With you and him."

"Nothing." She tried to say it innocently.

"Nothing is going on? Nothing?" She twisted her mouth wryly. "You're going to tell me you have had that beautiful hunk of man flesh under this roof all this time and you haven't slept with him?"

She crossed her arms. "Well, no."

"No, you didn't, or no, you did?"

"No, I did."

Lynette's eyes narrowed. "Don't you think that was kind of dangerous?"

A sudden vivid and erotic vision rose in her mind, a vision of their first joining, the sun making her lids red, his hands and mouth on her body. "No," she whispered. "He's a man of good character." It sounded old-fashioned, and she was embarrassed, but didn't take it back.

"That's not what I mean, Molly. Not dangerous as in taking a knife and stabbing you. Dangerous as in, can you stand to have your heart broken so completely again?"

Molly moved to the window, lifted the curtains and stared out. "My heart is fine," she lied.

"It can't be, Molly. Remember who you're talking to here, okay? I've known you all your life. I remember the boys you used to fall for. The Medina brothers, remember, in second grade? And Toby Espinoza. Nobody was more shocked than me when you ended up with some big old galoot of a white guy."

Her fingers tightened on the curtain, and she remembered a story they'd both heard at a Girl Scout gathering once: *The old women say there is a face carved on the heart of every woman...*

"Alejandro is nothing like them."

"No," Lynette said, "he's everything a man should be. He's kind and good and smart and beautiful. And you are in love with him."

Molly swallowed. "I've been thinking so much about Tim," she said quietly. "Remembering all these things about him that I loved so much. His hands. He had freckles on the back of his hands. And he was so romantic in practical ways, you know?" She turned to look at her best friend. "I broke down one night, just remembering everything about him. It came flooding back, so hard, and I felt like I was going to die, it hurt so much. I wanted to die when he did. There just didn't seem to be any point in going on."

"I know you did, sweetie," Lynette whispered.

"But you know, I picked myself up and I kept going. I don't remember how, now." She brushed a tear away and breathed out slowly. "That night I lost it, Alejandro came to me and just held me. He washed my face." She looked at Lynette, suddenly terrified and overwhelmed. "That day that I found him, it wasn't him calling for his niece that made me hide him. He was just so beautiful I needed to look at him some more." The words came pouring out of her, bottled up for too long. "I never did anything like that before, and I didn't even think about it. I just brought him into my house, like some antique or a beautiful painting, so I could look at him."

Lynette chuckled and brushed Molly's hair back from her face. "Honey, I've looked at him, okay? He's a lot better than a painting."

''You know what I mean. I never did that. And then, he woke up and there was something so special about him that I couldn't let him go.'' She closed her eyes. ''And now he's in every corner of my life. He's changed everything, everything, and it's going to be like it always is, it's going to hurt to let him go, but if I don't, Lynette, if I don't—'' she swallowed. ''Right now, it hurts a little. Later, it would be more than I could stand.''

Lynette laid her head on Molly's shoulder. ''Not everybody has to bury their parents and their husbands, Molly. Some people live a long time.''

''But you never know, do you?'' Molly said, and she could not hold back her tears. ''There are no guarantees in this life.''

''No,'' Lynette said quietly. ''There aren't.'' She put her arms around Molly's shoulders and let her weep. ''I'm so sorry, Moll. I'm sorry I wasn't there for you this time. I'm sorry this got so out of hand. I'm…'' She stroked Molly's hair. ''I'm sorry. If it makes you feel any better, I think you're doing the right thing, letting him go.''

But maybe that wasn't what Molly wanted to hear. Clinging to Lynette, she could only think of the way Alejandro had washed her face with a cool rag, of the way his hands looked when he wrapped Josefina's small hand in his own.

After a moment, she found the rush of emotion subsiding, and lifted her head, a backwash of foolishness making her laugh a little. ''I must be PMSing bad, the way I've been losing it today.''

''Maybe,'' Lynette said. ''But maybe a lot has happened in a short time, too.'' She smiled. ''Either way, things will look a lot better a week from now.''

"Will they?"

"They will. Now go wash your face. I'm going to get some of that coffee you said is so great."

When the snow began to come down again in earnest, Josh and Lynette gathered their things to go. Molly and Alejandro both went to the door, as if it was their shared home.

Josh extended his hand to Alejandro. "Best of luck to you, man."

"Thank you."

Lynette hugged Molly. "It's almost over now," she whispered. "Hang in there." She pulled back, lifted her collar. "Call me tomorrow."

"I will." She waved, then closed the door against the cold night.

Alejandro stood where he'd been, his arms at his sides, an odd expression on his face. Noticing her gaze, he summoned a smile, half-hearted. "You are very tired tonight, eh?"

She thought of the bed, thought of him there—and knew there was no way on earth, no way she could let herself sleep with him again. "Yes," she said, knowing they spoke in code.

"There's one thing more I would like to do, if you are not too tired," he said.

"What?"

He held out his hand. "Come."

And one last time, she allowed herself to touch him, let him take her hand in his and lead her into the kitchen. The table was cleared of dishes, but the flowers and candles, now unlit, remained. "Are you Catholic, Molly?"

"Sort of," she answered. "Lapsed."

"Then you know about candles for the dead."

A ripple of concern moved in her. Warily she said, "Yes."

"Please," he said, gesturing. "Sit down.

"In my village, we have a feast for the dead on their day." He uncovered a dish filled with multicolored cookies and brought it back to the table, then poured more coffee, releasing the cinnamon steam into the air. "We eat all their favorite things, because we believe that they can see them and smell them. I made *posole* because it was my sister's favorite. And she liked these cookies, too."

A true bolt of fear went through her. "Alejandro, I don't—"

He put his hand on hers, firmly, holding her in place. "I know. It's not always easy, to think of them, the ones who are gone. But—" he lit a match and held the flame to the wick of a candle "—I like to do it anyway. It's only a day or two early. The spirits won't mind." He put the candle down. "This one is for my sister, Josefina's mother, Silvia."

Against her will, Molly felt herself softly snared by the flickering gold candle flame, by the lilting rise and fall of his voice. "Silvia was one year older than me. She loved these cookies. She loved anything American. She was very beautiful—Josefina looks like her very much." His long fingers touched the edge of the jar. "I love her."

He raised his head, lit another match. "These two are for my parents. My mother, who loved flowers and her patio. My papa—" he grinned "—who loved to make money."

The trio of lights danced on his dark eyes when he handed her the box of matches. For a moment, she hesitated, then opened the box and took out a match. From the remaining holders on the table, she chose a matched set of round red glasses, and lit the votives within, an odd calm settling over her. "These are for my parents," she said, and her voice was strong. "My mother will be loving the smell of this coffee, and my father will be snorting over this foolishness, even though it pleases him to be remembered."

She looked at Alejandro, and he waited patiently, his hands resting easily on his long thighs, then she lifted one finger and went to the fridge, took out one of the beers her brother had left behind and carried it back to the table.

Amid the mostly glass candle holders was one carved of pine, one she'd picked up at a church bazaar one Christmas. Molly moved it in front of her, and opened the box of matches before she could chicken out, then lit it and held the match to the unburned wick. It caught and flared in a wide, wax-fed blaze, then settled into a steady yellow flame. She shook out the match.

"This one is for Tim," she said, and as if he heard his name, the essence of him filled her. It was not a sad feeling, but a joyous one, and she touched her chest in wonder. "He smelled of wood chips and soap." She opened the beer. "He loved beer and making things with his hands." A sweetness moved in her. "He was sturdy and strong and he loved this land with all his heart. Almost as much as he loved me."

Alejandro listened, a gentleness on his face. "He would have liked you very much, Alejandro. You could have talked roosters." Some of those tears, the ones she thought must be finished by now, slipped over her face, and she left them, because he would have liked that, too. "I loved him. I miss him a lot sometimes, still."

Alejandro leaned over the table and took her hand. "You *love* him. The dead, they never leave us. Not as long as we remember." And suddenly he picked up a cookie. "For Silvia!" he said, and mugged eating it with great gusto.

"For Tim!" she said, and took a great swig of beer, drinking it as he would have, in a big thirsty swallow, once, twice, three times. Some spilled over the side of her mouth, and she laughed, wiping it away with the back of her hand. "I'll have to practice that part."

He made a face at the cookies. "I never liked these very much."

"Oh, I do! I'll eat them for her." She reached for them and put one in her mouth, and ate it. "Thank you, Alejandro. For everything. The dinner tonight, and this." The entire evening had broken down her walls, and she said impulsively, "I'm really going to miss you. You've changed my whole life."

He bowed his head, as if the words pained him.

"I'm sorry," Molly said. "I didn't mean to make you uncomfortable. Forget I said anything."

"No, I want to remember." He gave her a somehow wistful expression. "I want to remember all of these days we have had here."

For one long moment, she ached to close the distance between them. She even saw herself, in her mind, kneeling before him, touching his face, kissing his hands, saw it so clearly it was almost as if she'd done it. But there was, tonight, an odd sort of distance between them, and it was impossible to reach over it, as it would have been to kiss a stranger in public. "So do

I,'' she said, and then, hesitantly, ''Alejandro, are we making a mistake?''

He stood, his face closed. ''No mistake, Saint Molly. This is best.'' He blew out the candles, all of them. ''For both of us.''

Chapter 15

Josh couldn't sleep, but it wasn't for the same reasons that had caused his insomnia the past week or so. Confession evidently was as good for the soul as they always said, because stating out loud that he'd been the one who fired a gun into a group of terrified migrant workers had eased his conscience. It still shamed him, but it wasn't festering in the same way tonight.

It also helped, he thought wryly, looking out to the piles of snow in his yard, that the guy hadn't died.

No, what kept him awake tonight was his sister. The funny light-struck expression in her eyes whenever she looked at Alejandro. Over and over, he played one moment: when they'd been at the stove, moving easily around each other as if they'd been married a hundred years. Then Molly had put her hand on his sleeve and lingered there. In that moment, the tall Mexican had looked at Molly as if she'd hung the damned moon.

And just for a second, Josh had seen the same thing in his sister's eyes.

Love. Not a mistake. Not for show. Not even admitted, he thought.

The clincher had been when Alejandro spoke to him about the house. That falling-down old white elephant Molly had been in love with as long as Josh could remember. Alejandro wanted her to have the house so she would have something that belonged to her. So she wouldn't—how had he put it?—*go hollow.*

Stirring sugar into a cup of tea, he pursed his lips. Hollow. That was such a damned good word for the way Molly had been since Tim died. The only time she'd really come alive was when she started on that house again, wanting to buy it and fix it up. But Josh, too, had been grieving his brother-in-law, and it hurt him that Molly would leave the land she and Tim had bought together.

Damn, but he was a self-centered SOB at times. Stubborn and stupid and sure he had all the answers. Guilt moved in him over his part in the separation of Molly from Alejandro. What right had he had to do that?

He'd make it right in the morning. Whether she knew it or not, Molly was crazy in love, and with a man who deserved her. Who would take good care of her. Who worshiped the ground she walked on. He'd call the sheriff—

Cut it out, a voice said wryly. What he had to do was step back and stop meddling. Let Molly make her own decisions. Claim her life—ask for what she wanted.

He could do that. But he suspected she might need

at least a nudge. He'd beat her down pretty hard this time. The least he could do was fix that part.

She could take it from there.

Josefina could not believe the sight outside her windows when she woke up. There was snow. Tons of it. Piles and piles, and more of it coming out of the sky. She wanted to go out and play in it so bad!

It took awhile for her to notice the other thing: it was quiet in the hospital. And the lights were not on. In surprise, she looked at the machines with their tubes and blinking lights and bleeping noises, and they were still, too. A nurse hurried in, frowning, though she brightened when she saw Josefina was awake. "How you doing, sweetie?"

"Good. Look at all the snow!"

"Yeah," she said, and didn't sound happy about it. "Three feet and it's still coming down." Quickly, she disconnected the machines and, giving Josefina warning, pulled the needle out of her arm and put a bandage on it. A pink one with doll faces.

"Am I going home now?"

"In a little while." She rolled up the various tubes. "The electricity is off in here and the machines won't work right. We have a generator to make electricity, but it's not working the way we want it to. There are some people who are really sick, and we have to save the power for their machines."

"Oh! I'm not so sick now."

The nurse patted her hand. "I know." She bustled out.

They brought her a breakfast that was cold. Kinda cold, anyway. Cereal and milk that tasted as though it might have been sitting on the counter for a little while.

Still, she found she was hungry enough for a bear, and ate all of it. When she was finishing up, a man came to her door.

She frowned. He did not wear a uniform, but she thought of a policeman, anyway. But he was pretty nice. "Hi, Josefina. I'm Molly's brother. Can I come in and talk to you for a minute?"

She nodded, deciding to wait and see what he had to say.

He had on a heavy coat with sheep fur on the inside. He had another one in his hands, littler, and she got scared, afraid it was for her. "What do you want?" she said, mean as she could.

"I need your help, kiddo."

"With what?"

"It's kind of secret. Let me ask you something, first. Do you like Molly?"

"Yes," she said fervently. "Does she like me?"

His smile was nice, Josefina decided. "Oh, yeah. She talks about you all the time. And about your uncle."

Josefina giggled. "She likes him a lot!"

"I know. He likes her, too."

"No," Josefina said gravely. "Tío is in love."

He made that expression grown-ups always got when they thought they were so much smarter than kids. "Really," he said. "What makes you think so?"

Now she wasn't so sure she wanted to tell him. He might just laugh at her, and she knew what she knew. "Lots of things."

"Like what?" When she didn't answer, he sat on the edge of her bed. "It's important, Josefina." He said her name wrong, but Anglos did that a lot. Like they were embarrassed to say it right.

"Ho-se-*FEE*na," she said.

"Oh. Sorry." He said her name again, right this time.

"Okay, this is how I know Tío is in love. One." She held up a finger. "He kissed her. He does not kiss women, not ever, even when there is a dance and they really want him to, bad. He says kissing leads to other things."

The man nodded, a little frown on his face. "I see. He's right."

"Two." Another finger. "He sang her the song about love. I don't know it in English, but he keeps that one for secret between us." Another finger. "He never stops looking at her when she's there. He tries to stop, but then he's doing it again. And there's so much happiness when he does."

The man was smiling now. "You know what, Josefina, that's exactly what I saw, too. And you know, my sister looks right back at him the same way." He got up and closed the door. "We have a problem, and you're gonna help me fix it."

"What problem? They got married."

He sighed. "I know. But it was only to get a green card."

"But they—"

"My turn to talk. I know. They're crazy in love. Loco," he said, and she smiled. "But they don't know it, so we have to help them find out."

"How?"

"We got lucky. You see that snow? My sister can't drive in it. Her truck got buried. So there they are, stuck."

Josefina grinned. "Ah-ha! So they probably have to kiss a little, huh?"

He laughed, and the sound was big and wide, like sunshine. Josefina liked him a lot better. "Exactly. You're pretty smart, for only being eight."

"I'm old for my age."

"Yeah." For some reason that seemed to make him sad. "Anyway. I have a better truck than my sister, and I can drive there. You get to get out of the hospital because they're worried about power failures, and I'm driving you up to Molly's house."

"Really? Is my dog there?"

"Not yet. He's still with Mr. Wiley. But listen, sugar. You and me, we're going to trick them, so they both see that they really are in love."

Josefina grinned. "Okay!"

Molly dreamed of a rooster. A big black one with a flare of red feathers at his chest, sitting on a fence post. For some reason, Tim was there, and her brother, Josh, and they were so happy to see the rooster, boasting about it. It was a Mexican rooster, they said, and very rare.

Behind them, she saw goats and sheep, and something green waving its fronds in the fields of her land. She frowned, confused. "I haven't planted anything. How did that happen?" she asked them, but they were already gone, and Molly was left to puzzle it out herself. The rooster crowed, and she turned to it, thinking he had the silkiest feathers she'd ever seen.

When she woke up, she half thought she'd heard the rooster, that it had been her alarm clock, and it took a long moment to realize it wasn't a rooster at all. It was the light.

Snow light. She sat up, surprised, and pulled open the curtains. "Holy cow!" she cried, half laughing, half appalled. Leo leaped up on the windowsill, his tail switching. "You won't be going outside today, my dear," she said to the cat. "You'd be buried."

The snow that had begun falling last night had evidently not ceased the entire night. It fell with deceptive sweetness, giant fluffy flakes, piling up. And up. And up. There was at least three feet in low spots, much more where the wind had piled it into drifts, and it showed no sign of slowing.

Secretly pleased—she loved these wild, surprise snows—she tugged on heavy socks and a pair of warm sweats and bundled her bathrobe around herself and went to make a pot of coffee. Padding silently down the hall, Leo rushing ahead to his food dish, she paused by Alejandro's half-open door to peak in. He slept, oblivious, his black hair scattered over the linens. She found herself smiling, thinking how lucky it was that fate had sent the snow today, so she could keep him a little longer. The phrase made her smile—keep him. Like Josefina's dog. *Please can I keep him?*

Silly. She shook her head, smiling, and went to make the coffee, moving quietly so she wouldn't disturb him. Although he seemed to possess an almost superhuman constitution, sleep was the body's way of repairing itself, and there was still a lot of healing going on in Alejandro's body.

As she fed Leonardo and waited for the coffee, she looked out the windows and thought about the rooster. In the bold light of morning, she had to chuckle a little at the imagery—a black rooster with red chest feathers. *Gee, wonder who that could be?* Certainly not Alejandro, with his black hair and red shirt. The only thing the rooster had lacked was a guitar.

Crossing her arms, she stood before the glass door

and saw the land the way it had appeared in her dream: fertile, productive, *alive*. Alive with sunshine and growing things and animals. In comparison, the dullness of empty fields filled with cactus seemed almost criminal, and for the first time, she understood how Tim and Alejandro viewed the potential of the land.

And Josh.

Josh. Of course. He was struggling so desperately to make ends meet, the kind of grueling, day-to-day struggle that wore a man out too soon, made him bitter and small. She'd seen the tension of it in his face often the past couple of years, and had repeatedly offered to help him—give him money, pay off his mortgage, whatever was best. Pridefully, he refused everything.

But if he worked the land, it would be the labor of his own back that would bring security. As much as possible anyway. She thought of what Alejandro had said about self-sufficiency. Maybe the land would never make a fortune, as Sunshine Farms and Wiley Farms, but at the very least, it could provide chickens and eggs and food of all kinds. It could bring in some extra money to be set aside for emergencies and eventually college for the kids.

She heard a step behind her, and Alejandro emerged, his hair tousled, his torso bare. She beamed at him. "Good morning!" she said, and without a single hesitation, she moved across the room, put her hands on his chest to brace herself and kissed him full on the mouth.

He was startled, but sleepy enough he didn't immediately protest. His hands went to her arms, and he gave her a quizzical look. "Molly?"

"It will wait," she said, and gestured toward the view. "Look! We're snowed in!"

He blinked at the brightness, and a hand went to his chest. "It snowed a lot!"

"And still coming down." She heard the gurgling of the coffeemaker. "Go wash up and I'll get some coffee."

Humming under her breath, she pulled out the makings for pancakes and stirred together dry ingredients, a sense of complete rightness in her. Josh and Lynette, Tim and Alejandro, the old house in town and the puzzle of her own land—all of it seemed so perfectly clear this morning that she couldn't imagine how she'd missed seeing it before.

Alejandro came back, buttoning his red shirt. She grinned at that, and he stopped. "What?"

She gave him a cup of coffee. "I'm just happy this morning. I was thinking about my brother and my land. He loves to work the land. He and Tim were going to do it together."

"A good idea. You need more than one man for so much land."

"Yeah, but when Tim died, I didn't even think of that. I didn't think about why Josh wanted me to go on with the farm." She shook her head. "I feel so selfish, but I was just not thinking all that clearly." She cut pieces of butter and put them in a bowl to melt in the microwave, then turned. "You were so right about the potential that's out there. I don't have to work the land myself. My brother can do it."

He still looked a little confused. Pulling out a chair, he sat down and took his socks from his back pocket. Then scowled as he realized the tops didn't match. Molly chuckled. "Check the corner over there. Leo probably stole your sock."

As if he heard his name, Leo dashed out, grabbed

the sock Alejandro had dropped on the floor and picked
it up in his teeth. Alejandro laughed and tugged on the
sock, taking it away, then dangling it in the air before
he tossed it, in a ball, across the room. Leo, tail switching, raced after it, retrieved it and brought it back to
Alejandro, who laughed, low in his chest. The half-
moon shine of teeth showed, and his eyes crinkled a
little and Molly thought he was going to be a very
dashing old man. When he looked up, his eyes were
dancing with that zest and life she found so appealing.
"A cat who fetches. His name should be Spot."

Everything narrowed to this minute. Finding a courage she didn't know she possessed, she said, "Alejandro?"

Hearing the shift in her tone, he looked up from his
game with Leo and sobered.

"Will you stay? Make the land what it should be,
work with my brother, show him what you know?"

His head bowed. "I cannot do that, Molly. I do not
wish to cause—"

"No, it wouldn't be like that. My brother will be so
glad to work the land that he won't care who does it
with him. And Josefina could have a solid place here."

He said nothing, only listened, a stillness in his body.
His eyes were deep, his mouth sober.

She met that liquid gaze, and bit her lip. Her heart
pounded a little in fear and hope. "Alejandro, can we
be practical here?"

His mouth turned down at the corners, as if he had
not expected that word, but it was okay. "Sure."

She took a breath, remembering what he'd said about
the women in his village, the ones who would have
valued him as a husband. "I value your strong back
and your good financial sense. I'm strong, too. And I

have land to offer as my dowry.'' She managed a little chuckle. ''Isn't that how it's done?''

He looked troubled. ''Molly—''

She held up a hand. ''Let me finish, okay? I don't know if I'll ever be able to offer you more children, but as you said, there are many children who need homes, and I would be willing to bring some of them in if you need that in your life.'' She found her hand pressing against her ribs, and noticed that her fingers hurt with the pressure. ''I'm a widow and I'm lonely, and I don't want to live alone anymore. We get along well. There is something good when we have sex. It seems to me that there would be worse things for both of us than to just—'' her voice croaked a little ''—stay married.''

His lids fell, hiding his eyes, and Molly thought there was a burn of color on his cheekbones. ''Practical, eh?''

''Is that wrong? I don't want you to feel you have to give me some promise of undying love or something.''

''Practical,'' he said again, and stood. He wore an odd expression, both fierce and hurt, as he crossed the room and stopped in front of her. She looked up, sensing she'd done something wrong, but completely bewildered as to what it might be, how she had offended him.

''I am a practical man,'' he said. ''I see your bargain is a wise one for both of us.'' But he shook his head. ''But I am not practical in matters of love, Saint Molly.'' His eyes burned, molten again, hot as lava, and he lifted his hands to her hair, letting it trail through his fingers. ''My heart is bound to magic. My soul needs wonder.'' He grasped her head in his hands and lifted her face to his kiss. A slow, knee-buckling kiss.

He lifted his head again, and there was a sad smile on his mouth. "You see, Saint Molly, I am not a man who loves lightly. There is too much passion in me, I think, and so I don't let it out." He shook his head, brushed his thumb over her mouth. "I cannot be the man you wish. That practical one. I wish I could."

Her heart swelled, and before he could move away, she captured his wrists with her hands, holding him there. "I believe in magic, Alejandro," she said softly. "There's a story that the old women tell, of the face that's carved on the heart of a woman. Every woman. It's a story they use to warn young girls to be careful with themselves." She swallowed, moved her hands to his face and whispered, "When I found you that morning, I saw the face that was carved into my heart." Holding his gaze, she said, "Everything I've done since then was because of that."

Alejandro stared down at her for a long, long moment, a rush of something unnamed, unknown till now, moving through his body. It was dizziness and pleasure and passion, and such vast, intense relief that he did the only thing he could: he made a sound and kissed her. Kissed her mouth and her face, her eyes and her neck, his need urgent and carnal. In the cold kitchen, he untied her robe and tugged up her nightgown and kissed her breasts. He cradled her hips and hauled her hard against him. As if his passion kindled hers, they shed as many clothes as they needed, and without moving anywhere, joined together leaning against the sink. Only then, when he was buried in her, her naked breasts against his chest, her mouth open to his, could he speak. He lifted his head and looked into her ghostly eyes, silvery now with passion, and said, *"Te amo, Molly. I love you."* He closed his eyes, feeling the words too small to express what he felt, and kissed her and hauled her closer, *"Te amo."*

She kissed his cheekbones, his nose, his mouth, touched his forehead, his hair. "I love you, Alejandro."

And they joined with holy carnality, laughing when they slipped and nearly fell, and slid to the floor to finish, and in spite of the cold floor, in spite of the awkwardness, they swelled together, and both of them were weeping when it was done.

Alejandro rested his forehead in the curve of her neck, and breathed his thanks to the fates. To his sister, to his father, to the fall of the Mexican economy, to Josh for shooting him, to everything that had played whatever tiny part in bringing him here, to this woman. His woman.

His wife.

The sound of a huge engine sounded outside, and they both startled, then skittered apart when a knock came on the door. "Just a minute," Molly cried out, and dissolved in laughter when she tangled the leg of her sweats inside out. Alejandro shoved his hair out of his face and fastened his jeans. Leaving his shirt unbuttoned for the moment, he helped Molly up, smoothing her gown down, widening his eyes in laughter.

"Knock, knock!" Josh called from the living room. "Special delivery!"

Molly shook her hair out of her face and looked up at Alejandro, as if asking his approval. She had a red mark on her neck, bold and plain, and touched it, shrugging.

"What are we going to tell him?" she whispered to Alejandro. "In here!" she called out.

Josh carried his shrouded bundle carefully. She wasn't heavy—in fact she was almost painfully light. But the cold air was a danger to her lungs, and the hospital had fretted over it. He promised to keep her head and face covered and Josefina had promised to follow orders exactly. So now, she curled in his arms, her blanket up over her nose. "You can take it off now, honey," he said.

"Is this my house?" she whispered urgently, her eyes wide.

"Yep." He heard a sound of giggles, quickly hushed, and slowed just a bit. "You know what?" he said, stopping entirely.

"What?"

"Maybe we aren't going to have to do any tricks." He grinned as another throaty, satisfied laugh came from the kitchen, and a sound of scuffling, and the lower laugh of a man. "What do you think?"

Josefina gave him an impish, knowing grin. "Put me down."

So Josh was trailing behind a strong little girl who strode down his sister's hallway in her bunny slippers, and he had a chance to observe it all. Molly, her hair a mess all over her shoulders, her sweats on inside out, her feet bare and a love bite on her neck the size of Texas. Alejandro, his hair even wilder than Molly's, his shirt buttoned crookedly.

It was the expression they both wore that got him, though. Flushed and beaming. And then—

"Hi, Tío," Josefina said, and held out her hands. "Here I am."

If there had been even the slightest of lingering doubts in Josh's mind about Alejandro Sosa, they were erased in that instant. The man, plainly overwhelmed, simply fell to his knees and opened his arms. Tears streamed down his dark face as he hugged the little girl. "Welcome to your new home, *hija*," he whispered against her hair. "Welcome home." He turned to Molly, who had crouched beside them, his eyes shining, and kissed her, in front of the world and Josh and his niece.

"Uh, Josh," Molly said. "There's been a change of plan?"

Josefina reached out a tiny hand and put it on Molly's shoulder. "Don't worry, Molly. He knows you are in love."

For one moment, Molly stared at him, obviously worried. He crossed the room and hugged her. "I knew last night, kiddo."

He turned and held out a hand to his brother-in-law. "Congratulations."

But Alejandro snared him with his free arm and gave him a hug. A little surprised, Josh resisted at first, then realized it felt pretty damned good to be included. To be inside, to have family who cared, and he managed to hug a little in return.

"Thank you, brother," Alejandro said.

Epilogue

Molly could scarcely contain her impatience. She had been to the window a dozen times in ten minutes, peering out to the road, and pacing back into the kitchen. The little scruffy dog, a ratty terrier mix, followed her back and forth. Josefina finally took her by the hand and said, "We should maybe wait on the porch, huh?"

Molly laughed. "Yes."

But as they stepped outside to the brilliant spring day, Molly squealed. "There it is!" She pointed, and even found herself jumping up and down in her excitement. "Look!"

Even Josefina was impressed. Her mouth dropped. "It's so big!"

"Yes it is."

The crew of construction workers across the way heard the engines and all of them stopped, too, to watch the rare spectacle of a house moving down the road, turrets and all. The windows were boarded carefully, and the road had had to be widened, and even then, it took a whole contingent of cars before and behind to keep the passage free for the huge moving job.

As it lumbered toward the foundation waiting for it, Molly sank onto the steps and covered her mouth.

"Why are you crying, Mama Molly?"

Molly brushed the tears off her face. "I'm happy," she said. "Did you ever want something so bad and you were just sure you would never get it, and then you did?"

Josefina nodded, very soberly. Her hand moved on her dog's head.

"That's how I feel about that house. I've wanted to live in it since I was just a little bit older than you."

Josefina looked at it nervously. "I like my room now, though."

"I know." She took her hand. "You like the curtains, but I promise I can move them into a new room when we get it done." She pointed. "You see that round part, with windows all around?"

"That's going to be my room?" Josefina guessed, and looked at Molly with wide eyes. "Like a princess?"

Molly laughed in delight. "Exactly like a princess."

Alejandro jumped from a truck in order to direct the driver to level ground. He waved his hat wildly at Molly and Josefina, and even over the noise, they could hear his cry, "Whooo—eee!"

"Molly?"

Grinning, she looked down at the little girl. "Yes?"

"I think I'm already the princess. And you're the queen, and Tío is the king."

Molly laughed, a warmth and richness in her heart. "You know what? I think you're right."

Josefina sighed. "Everything is going to be just fine."

"Just fine," Molly agreed.

Never perfect, but always just fine. Life was full of miracles.

*   *   *   *   *

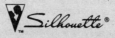

If you enjoyed what you just read,
then we've got an offer you can't resist!

Take 2 bestselling love stories FREE!

Plus get a FREE surprise gift!

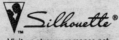

In December 1999
three spectacular authors invite you to share the
romance of the season as three special gifts are

Delivered by Christmas

A heartwarming holiday anthology featuring

BLUEBIRD WINTER
by *New York Times* bestselling author

Linda Howard

A baby is about to be born on the side of the road. The single
mother's only hope rests in the strong arms of a dashing doctor....

And two brand-new stories:

THE GIFT OF JOY
by national bestselling author **Joan Hohl**

A bride was not what a Texas-Ranger-turned-rancher was
expecting for the holidays. Will his quest for a home lead to love?

A CHRISTMAS TO TREASURE
by award-winning author **Sandra Steffen**

A daddy is all two children want for Christmas. And the
handsome man upstairs may be just the hero their mommy needs!

*Give yourself the gift of romance in
this special holiday collection!*

Available at your favorite retail outlet.